CALORIC

TRICIA BARR

Tici Ben

CHAPTER 1

Consciousness came slowly this morning for Phoenyx Blake. Blurry, dreamy images flashed in her reluctantly waking mind—images that didn't make sense. She had vague memories of being carried, as if over a strong man's shoulder. *Did I really have that much to drink last night?* Come to think of it, she couldn't remember much at all of the night before. Her head was aching fiercely, an incentive to stay asleep as long as she could. However, her aching back made it too difficult to sleep any longer.

She opened her eyes, the fuzzy world coming more into focus with each blink.

She didn't expect what she saw. There was a bright florescent light overhead—attached to a dark gray cement ceiling—creating an illusion of darkness despite the light. As her eyes wandered, she saw thick metal rods descending from the ceiling to one side of her. Her other senses came into focus, making her aware of the scents of dust and mildew, and of the frigid chill that clung to her bare arms and rose prickly goosebumps. Fear suddenly struck her as she realized she was in some kind of jail cell.

She sat up quickly, her hands rushing to her head to fight the dizziness her quick movement caused.

"You're awake," a soft female voice said next to her.

Phoenyx removed her hands to see a girl about her age sitting in the corner of the cell to her right. Her arms were wrapped around her knees.

"I tried to wake you earlier but you were out cold," the girl said in a timid voice.

Phoenyx took a moment to scrutinize the girl. Her long, curly brown hair was the color of tree bark fresh off an oak tree. Her large eyes were very green, like fresh spring grass. Her small, round and sweetly pretty face was scrunched by worry at the moment and streaked with pale lines as though she had been crying. She was wearing jeans, a plain white T-shirt, and gray tennis shoes.

"Wh...where are we?" Phoenyx asked, trying to make sense of her surroundings.

She looked around. They were in a small square room, all four walls and the floor the same gray cement as the ceiling. There was a row of iron bars dividing the room, and another perpendicular to that meeting up halfway, creating two small cells, each with a toilet against the wall. They were in the right cell and the left one was empty. Across from the cells was one heavy-looking door. There were no windows in this room. There weren't even air vents.

A rush of emotions hit her. Claustrophobia because this tiny place had no apparent means of escape; confusion and a sense of violation because she woke in a strange place; and fear for why she was brought here.

"I really don't know," the girl said, creasing her brow and sniffling. "It's pretty obvious this isn't a legal holding cell. I can't remember a thing about how I got here but I'm sure this isn't what being arrested is like— not that I've done anything wrong anyway. I have been awake for about," she paused to look at the watch on her wrist, "three hours and no one has come through that door."

The girl broke down and cried fresh tears. "I'm sorry." She wept. "I'm just so scared."

Shaking, Phoenix stood up and moved to sit beside the weeping girl. She had an overwhelming need to comfort her, despite her own growing anxiety.

"What's the last thing you remember?" Phoenyx asked, as of yet unable to answer that question herself.

The girl wiped away her tears and shook her head. "I hardly remember anything. I guess the last thing I remember is digging in my garden." The girl sniffed loudly, then looked at Phoenyx. "What about you?"

Phoenyx closed her eyes and tried hard to remember. She went back farther in her memory, deciding to trace events forward rather than backward. She had been accepted into UCLA. She and her mother decided it would be best for her to move to Los Angeles before the school year started so she could get acclimated to the city. She had been in L.A. for two weeks and stayed in an apartment she rented only for the month, expecting to move into the dorms on campus when school started. Since this was her last few weeks of summer, she made good use of her fake ID. Not that she really needed one.

Now she was getting closer. She distinctly remembered going to a bar and flirting with a cute guy who bought her a drink. He asked a lot of strange questions, too personal, so she excused herself and left...walking out of the bar was as far as her memory went before fading to black. She realized what must have happened. The way her head ached and felt so heavy and foggy, this was no hangover—she must have been drugged.

"The last thing I remember is being at this bar," Phoenyx said. "Some guy was buying me drinks and being kind of creepy, so I walked out. I'm pretty sure he must have slipped something into my drink somehow."

The girl cringed at the thought, far more concerned now.

Phoenyx searched around in her pockets and came out with her cell phone—which was dead—her fake ID, and a folded up bar napkin. She put the useless phone and ID card on the floor and handed the napkin to the girl.

"Thank you," the girl said, taking the napkin and blowing her nose. "I'm Lily, Lily Taylor," she offered. "I would say it's nice to meet you but, under the circumstances..."

Phoenyx nodded understandingly. "I'm Phoenyx Blake."

"Phoenix, that's a clever name," Lily said, obviously trying to make small talk. "Because of your hair. Like the bird."

"Actually, I was named after the city in Arizona," Phoenyx corrected. "My mom grew up there and loved it. A lot of people assume as you did." She fingered a strand of her straight, chin-length, bright orange hair.

Lily nodded, looking distracted.

"Why do you think we are here?" Lily asked, picking nervously at the napkin. "What do you think he wants with us?"

Phoenyx's heart jumped into her throat. She attempted to swallow the lump away.

"Whatever it is, it can't be good," she said. "We can only hope we are being *Punk'd*." She smirked, trying to lighten the very dark mood in the air.

Lily laughed, grateful for the light-hearted suggestion, though neither of them really believed that could be the case.

Phoenyx stood and inspected their prison. The bars were firmly secured to the walls, ceiling, and floor. She moved to the cell door and looked for any flaw in the lock. Unfortunately, this wasn't the kind of lock that took a regular key, the kind that could be easily picked with a hair pin. It appeared to be card-activated. She grabbed the bars of the door and shook them as hard as she could but the door didn't give in the slightest.

"You don't happen to have any Jackie Chan type martial arts training, do you?" Phoenyx asked. "Or happen to be an expert locksmith?"

"I'm afraid not," Lily said. "I'm just a simple nursing student."

"Oh, do you go to UCLA, too?" Phoenyx asked.

Lily looked perplexed. "Umm, no. I go to the University of Washington."

"Oh...so you are in L.A. on vacation?" Phoenyx asked.

As if putting the pieces together simultaneously, they both shook their heads.

"I was in L.A. and you were in Seattle," Phoenyx thought aloud. "For whatever reason, we were brought to the same place."

She sighed and started pacing. "This situation was scary enough when this seemed like a random abduction and when I thought we were still in L.A. We could be *anywhere* if someone went through all the trouble to cross state lines. The fact that you and I are from completely different states means we weren't taken at random, right? What could anyone want with us specifically?"

Lily shook her head and put her chin on her knees.

Phoenyx put her head against the bars and let the hoard of fretful thoughts run rampant in her mind. *Why would anyone do this? What could anyone possibly want with two simple girls from two different states?* They were both pretty, attractive girls. Could they be victims of human trafficking? White hot panic flushed through her veins like a poison at the thought. *No, no, don't get too frantic yet.* There were only two of them here. If this was human trafficking, wouldn't there be more girls? They weren't harmed in any way. Not that she was an expert on sex trading, but she wouldn't expect the kind of men who partake in that business to be gentle.

So, what could it be then? Phoenyx never committed even so much as petty theft and, as far as she knew, she hadn't made any enemies. In fact, making people like her was her *special skill*. Whenever she wanted something from someone, all she had to do was touch them and they would do anything she asked. That was why she didn't really need a fake ID to get into bars, she could just brush her hand on the bouncer's arm and they would let her in without a second thought. The ID just served as insurance.

Insurance...what about ransom? No, that wasn't likely either. Her mom had very little money. It was only because of her dad's life insurance that she could afford college. She couldn't say the same about Lily, but their captors wouldn't get much for Phoenyx.

She turned around and looked at Lily, who was casually looking at the ID card Phoenyx had left on the floor.

"So, you're twenty-one huh?" Lily asked, trying to fill the silence. "Is it the big deal everyone makes it out to be?"

Phoenyx smirked coyly. "Actually, that's a fake ID. I'm only nineteen. Just turned nineteen on June sixth."

Lily's brow furrowed and she looked taken aback. "That's my birthday too."

Phoenyx shook her head in disbelief. "No way."

"Yes," Lily insisted.

She reached in her back pocket and pulled out a small wallet. She removed her ID and handed it to Phoenyx. The plastic card verified that they really did have the same birthday.

"This is too much of a coincidence," Phoenyx said. "What significance could our birth date have to anyone? This makes absolutely no sense to me."

She gave the ID back to Lily.

"We have to find some way out of here," Lily said, sounding more determined than frightened.

Phoenyx thought for a moment.

"Someone has to come in here eventually," she said.

She sat down beside Lily once more and lowered her voice. "The minute someone opens the cell door, we kick and scratch and bite and do whatever we have to do to—"

She was cut off by the loud clinking sound of the heavy door being unlocked. The two girls shared a quick understanding look, then fixed their eyes to the door. It opened with a rude creak and a large, bulky bald man entered the room.

Of course, he would have to be a huge guy, wouldn't he? As if they weren't already up a creek without a paddle.

They stared at him cautiously, waiting. The second he opened the cell door they were prepared to attack him in whatever way possible.

He didn't go anywhere near the cell door. He regarded them for a moment where he stood. Then, without taking a step closer, he tossed a paper bag at the base of the cell, turned around, and walked out, closing and locking the door once more.

Phoenyx and Lily exchanged surprised, suspicious glances, hesitating before either made a move toward the paper bag. They reached out for it together and looked inside. It contained two bottles of water, two apples, and two small McDonald's burgers.

"Well, at least we can be sure of one thing," Phoenyx said.

"What's that?" Lily asked.

"We're not dealing with a serial killer. He wouldn't have fed us if he was just going to kill us." The statement came out of her mouth like a joke but that scenario was a real possibility.

"I think we know something else, too," Lily said.

"What?"

"I assume that wasn't the guy harassing you in the bar because you didn't recognize him. If you're sure the guy from the bar was the one who drugged you, then we know there is more than one person involved in whatever is going on here. That makes any chance of escape much less likely."

They both sighed heavily and took the burgers out of the bag. The smell of warm, fresh burgers assaulted their nostrils.

"You don't think they would have tampered with these, do you?" Lily asked. Her stomach growled.

"Considering that we have no idea how long we are going to be in here, I don't think we have the choice not to eat them," Phoenyx said. "We either take the risk or starve."

Lily nodded, then eagerly unwrapped her burger and took a big bite out of it. Phoenyx followed suit and they continued eating in silence.

Phoenyx spent the day exploring downtown L.A., basking in the aromatics of the flower district, window shopping to her heart's content in the clothing district and narrowly avoiding one particularly impatient driver at a crosswalk. She made sure to leave that area before sunset, as she had been told by some friendly locals that downtown is a dangerous place at night—cops won't even patrol downtown at night.

Now, after a long day of walking, she wanted to rest her feet and get a drink. She had been to a few nightclubs here and none of them were all that interesting. The people were all so phony and pretty rude. That must just be the type of people a big city produces. She would much rather go to a cozy little bar—maybe one with a pool table and cold beer on tap. There was one a bit down the street from her apartment which was hole-in-the-wall enough. Perhaps she should try that.

She went home, cleaned up, and dressed up a little. She took one last look in the mirror as she always did before leaving to go out in public. Her bob cut orange hair was perfectly straight and shiny; her almond-shaped amber-colored eyes perfectly lined and smoky. Satisfied, she locked up and headed down to the bar. She decided not to take her purse because it was too much of a bother. She just brought her cell phone, her ID, and a twenty dollar bill.

She walked inside the quaint little place and took a seat at the bar. The bartender was a middle-aged blond woman with sun damaged skin left bare by a spaghetti strap shirt. When the woman saw Phoenyx, she raised an eyebrow and sauntered over.

"I'm afraid I'm gonna have to see some ID," she said with a sharp, twangy Texan accent.

Phoenyx lightly placed her hand on top of the bartender's hand that rested on the bar top. As she had done so many times before, she let her will flow through her hand. It wasn't really something she could explain, but the feeling was always of a sensual nature. Somehow that sensual energy passed from her to the person she was touching, causing that person to melt like putty in her hands and want nothing more than to do what she asks.

The bartender's hard sternness instantly relaxed, her shoulders dropping ever so slightly. Phoenyx couldn't be sure due to the bartender's sun darkened complexion, but she almost appeared to be blushing.

"No you don't," Phoenyx said softly, with her hand still on the bartender's. "Isn't it obvious I'm over twenty-one?"

"Of course, darlin'," the bartender said, smiling fondly. "What can I getcha?"

"Whatever you have on tap," Phoenyx replied.

"Comin' right up," the bartender said and went to fix the drink.

"That was a pretty nifty trick," a man's voice said from down the bar top.

Phoenyx looked in that direction. The man was fairly handsome, somewhere in his mid-twenties, with clean cut short brown hair. Odd, she couldn't recall seeing anyone at the bar when she first sat down. He was dressed plainly enough, in a simple blue T-shirt and black jeans, but something about the way he held himself gave off a sense of propriety and privilege.

He got up from his stool and moved to sit next to her.

"How old are you really?" he asked. "It'll be our little secret," he whispered.

She found his bravado amusing so she decided to indulge him.

"Nineteen," she said in a hushed voice.

"Ah, and let me guess, you're a...Gemini?"

"Yes, actually," she said. "How could you tell?"

He shrugged and said, "I have a gift for these things."

The bartender came back and set the tall frosty beer in front of Phoenyx. Before Phoenyx could retrieve any cash, the man handed the bartender a five dollar bill as payment for the beer.

"Let me know if you need anything else," the bartender said.

"Thank you," Phoenyx said, and the bartender smiled and walked away.

"My name is Dex," the man said. "Who do I have the pleasure of buying a drink?"

Silently remarking at his, for this city, peculiarly great manners, she replied, "My name is Phoenyx. Spelled with a Y instead of an I. My mother felt it was more feminine that way."

He chuckled.

"What's funny?" she asked, feeling like he was laughing at her rather than with her.

"Oh, just that life can be so ironic at times," he said, flashing a charming smile. "I promise you'll get the joke later. Now tell me, what is a girl like you doing in the city of Lost Angels?"

"What makes you think I'm not from here?" she asked before taking a sip of her beer.

"Like I said, I have a gift for these things," he answered.

She shrugged and said, "Okay? Well, I'm going to be starting at UCLA in a few weeks. I just moved here from Illinois. What about you?"

"I'm here on business," he said vaguely.

She nodded, noting he was being purposefully ambiguous and she was losing her interest because of it. She eyed him as she took another drink and saw a unique pin on his shirt. It was square shaped and had a different color box at each corner, one red, one yellow, one blue and one green. It almost looked like the Windows logo.

"That pin you're wearing," she said, "what's it for?"

"Oh," he said, momentarily taken aback. "I belong to a fraternity of sorts. I won't bore you with those details. I'm sure you'll meet plenty of frat boys at UCLA."

Now his dodginess was just becoming irritating.

He put his hand on hers and moved his thumb over the unsightly oblong scar that besmirched her otherwise pretty feminine wrist. Feeling like her space was being uninvitedly invaded, she pulled her hand back.

"Do you mind if I ask you how you got that scar?" Dex asked.

Phoenyx drank down her beer and then said, "Actually, I have an early morning. Thank you for the beer." She slid off her stool.

"Perhaps I'll see you again," he said cordially.

She wasn't sure if he was actually oblivious to her annoyance or just pretending to be.

"You never know," she said, smiled, and then headed for the door.

* * * *

"Phoenyx, what are you thinking about?" Lily asked, snapping Phoenyx out of her rumination.

"Oh, just replaying that night in my head," Phoenyx said. "Now that I can remember it more clearly, I guess I'm trying to look for any clues as to why we're here."

"Did you find any?" Lily asked.

Phoenyx shook her head.

Their night was miserable—not that they could really even tell it was night in this room. The only means they had of telling time was Lily's fancy wristwatch that showed, not only the time but, the date as well.

Neither of them had really slept. The cement floor was far too uncomfortable to lie down on, which was probably why her back hurt since she first woke up in this prison. They tried finding a way to sleep sitting up, but every echoed sound from outside this room made them startle to alertness. They finally gave up on sleep at 5:30 a.m. and spent the morning mostly in silence.

The burgers and apples yesterday didn't last long and now they were both pretty hungry. They decided it was best to conserve their water, as that was more important than food. Phoenyx hoped someone would bring them more food soon.

"I don't think I can bare the silence much more," Lily admitted. "We should talk about something."

"Like how good a steak sounds right now," Phoenyx said.

Lily laughed. "Well, maybe not that. No point in tormenting ourselves."

"That's a good point," Phoenyx agreed. "In that case, let's do what girls do best and talk about boys. You got a boyfriend back in Seattle?"

"No." Lily frowned and shrugged. "I don't really have time for one, with school and all my projects. The nursing program requires about eight hours of class a day, and that's not even including homework and study time."

"Yikes," Phoenyx said. "That's a hell of a work load."

"Do you have a boyfriend?" Lily asked.

"I had a boyfriend in high school for a little while but he was a real idiot. He ruined my prom night, and that was the last straw. I knew we weren't going to last long distance anyway, once I went off to college, so it was best that we broke it off early."

"Were you hoping to find a new boyfriend once you get to college?" Lily asked.

"I don't know." Phoenyx shrugged. "If I find someone interesting, I might give it a try, but I'm not going to seek one out. The best guys come around when you're not looking for them, you know. Or so I've heard anyway."

"I'll keep that in mind," Lily said. "You said you were going to UCLA, right? What do you study?"

"I don't really know yet, to be honest," Phoenyx said. "I haven't started yet. This was going to be my first year. Actually…" Phoenyx cocked her head at Lily, "didn't you say you were already going to UW? How is that—we're the same age?"

"I graduated high school a year early," Lily said. "I have always wanted to go into medicine, so I was really eager to start college right after. This is going to be my sophomore year."

"What made you want to be a nurse?" Phoenyx asked. "Personally, I'm kinda squeamish. If I ever see a drop of blood, I'm intensely disgusted."

Lily laughed. "That stuff doesn't bother me, at all. Well, not in that sense any way. The sight of blood, to me, means that someone is in pain; it just makes me more determined to help. I've always been that way, driven to help people. Nursing just seems like a way to do that; better than being a doctor anyway because they don't spend as much time with their patients. And private practice doctors are really just in it for the money."

"What's UW like?" Phoenyx asked.

"Beautiful," Lily responded, smiling briefly at the thought of it. "I joined the gardening club. Last spring, we made a huge effort to plant more trees and pretty gardens around campus. It's such a lovely place now."

"Gardening?" Phoenyx asked playfully. "Nursing and gardening—that's quite a mix of interests."

"I've always had a knack for gardening," Lily said. "I can bring just about any plant 'back from the dead', you could say." She used air quotes. "My Aunt Gene calls me Green Thumb."

"Aww, that's kinda cute," Phoenyx said.

"What's UCLA like? I mean, what you've seen of it?"

"It's a pretty campus," Phoenyx said. "And huge. I walked around last week to make sure I knew where all my classes were going to be and spent the whole day walking. Thankfully there's an hour gap between each of my classes."

"You have no idea what you want to study yet?" Lily asked.

"Not really. There's so much I'm interested in, but not that one thing I'm super passionate about. I'm hoping that sometime in the first year it will find me; although that may not even matter now." She instantly regretted saying that. It brought them both back into the reality of where they were, and neither of them wanted to be reminded of it. It was better to think about happy things and pretend they were anywhere else but here in this cell in this gloomy cement room.

"Sorry," Phoenyx said to the suddenly solemn Lily. "I didn't mean to be a buzz kill."

Lily shook her head. "It's okay. We were both thinking it."

They sat in a moment of awkward silence.

"You know, you would think they'd be decent enough to at least give us some music," Phoenyx complained.

Lily's brows jumped. "You know any good songs? We could create our own music."

"Yeah, okay. Do you know '*When I'm Gone*'? The cup song?"

"What self-respecting teen girl doesn't know that song?" Lily laughed.

Lily made the cup sounds with her half-empty water bottle in perfect rhythm, clapping it and hitting the ground with it.

"I got my ticket for the long way round," Phoenyx sang. "Two bottles of whiskey for the way. And I sure would like some sweet company and I'm leaving tomorrow, whad'ya say."

Lily added her voice. "When I'm gone, when I'm gone, you're gonna miss me when I'm gone. You're gonna—"

They were cut off by the *clickety clack* of the door being unlocked on the other side. The door opened and that same giant, bald man came in.

Feeling brave, without hesitation, Phoenyx jumped to her feet and pressed herself against the bars.

"What do you want with us?" she demanded.

As if not hearing her, or simply deeming her unworthy of acknowledgement, the man flung a similar brown paper bag at them, turned around, and walked out.

"Hey! You can't keep us locked up in here!" Phoenyx yelled after him.

The door clunked closed.

Grunting in futility, Phoenyx turned and slid her back down the bars until her butt touched the ground. She pulled the paper bag through the bars. The same things were in the bag as last time. Phoenyx tossed Lily one of the burgers.

Lily started singing again. After a verse, Phoenyx joined in. They sang together louder and louder, feeling less and less despaired. When the song was over, Phoenyx sang another song, and then Lily after that and so on. They took this dark, hopeless place and filled it with life and color. For that hour or two, they weren't completely miserable.

Sleep proved just as illusive tonight as it was the night before. Phoenyx fashioned a crude sort of pillow by crumpling up the two paper bags. If she lay on her side with her hands tucked between the side of her head and the bags, she wasn't too horribly uncomfortable. No matter how badly her body wanted to sleep, her mind couldn't rest. The horrible anxiety she successfully contained ate away at her insides. She tried to stay optimistic and strong for Lily's sake, but wasn't sure how long she had before her fears would devour her sanity.

Phoenyx missed her mom. Mom, who had no idea yet that her daughter was missing. Mom, whose cooking she pined for since she left—it wasn't as much fun as one might think to eat take out all the time. She wished she spent more time learning how to cook from her mom. She wished she spent more time with her in general.

She missed the sky. Even though it had only been two days in this dreary prison, two days that drug on like a broken clock with no cuckoo. The heat of the sun would feel so good right now. It used to be a sure fire way to put her to sleep, back when they lived in Arizona. Sitting on a lawn chair on the patio in the middle of summer, letting the sweet heat just smother her, it was almost suffocating. When she and her mother moved to Illinois, she could barely enjoy the sun for all the cold so coming to L.A. had been such a nice change. It was possible that L.A. was even hotter than Phoenix and she had loved it so far.

What she missed most of all, especially right now, was a bed with pillows and cushy blankets. Oh, and her kingdom for a damn light switch! If she could just turn out that stupid florescent light, she might be able to fall asleep for two seconds.

Sniff, sniff.

Phoenyx heard the softest sound coming from Lily's corner. She was crying. Phoenyx wasn't even aware that Lily was awake. She had been so quiet all this time. Probably only because she was doing the same thing Phoenyx was doing—dwelling.

Phoenyx crawled silently over toward Lily.

"Lily?" she asked softly.

Sniff, sniff, SNIFF!

"Phoenyx, you're awake?" Lily asked, sitting upright and wiping under her nose. "Did I wake you? I'm sorry."

"No, no, I couldn't sleep either," she said. "Are you okay?" What a stupid question to ask. Of course Lily wasn't okay. Nothing about this was okay.

Lily's face puckered up and turned red, then she really started balling. "No! I can't stop thinking about my mom and dad. They have to be so worried about me right now. I can just see them freaking out because I haven't been home in three days. I've never even been out after midnight before!"

Phoenyx put her hand on Lily's back and rubbed comfortingly.

"I know how you feel," Phoenyx said. "If this had happened while I was living at home, my mom would be freaking out too. At least your parents know you're missing so they will have a better chance of maybe finding us. My mom won't realize I'm missing for...geez, it could be weeks. When she calls me several times in a row and I don't answer, and then she calls the school and finds out I never checked in, then she'll know, and by then..." Phoenyx's throat tightened and her own eyes teared up. "By then, it might be too late."

"Phoenyx, what if we never get to see them again?" Lily sobbed.

"You shouldn't think like that," Phoenyx said.

"I can't help it," Lily said. "I don't know how to keep ignoring that we're trapped in here."

Phoenyx paused for a moment, struggling to swallow the lump in her throat. Then, all at once, reality came crashing down on her like a huge weight she couldn't hold up anymore. Her tears broke free in a real ugly cry.

Lily immediately and maternally threw her arms around Phoenyx and they cried together.

"I miss my mom!" Phoenyx cried. "I've been trying not to think about her, but I wish more than anything I was in her arms right now."

"Me, too," Lily cried. "I miss my dad and my baby sister. What if I never get to hug her again?"

They cried, their tears soaking each other, until the crying naturally sputtered out and the only thing to be heard was a symphony of sniffles.

"My dad always makes the world seem so small," Lily said quietly, breaking a long silence. "He's such a big guy; so strong, like nothing in the world can touch him or me when I'm with him."

"I remember feeling that way," Phoenyx said after a moment. "The feeling of being carried by my dad, so high up that nothing bad could reach me. I really miss him."

"What happened to your dad?" Lily asked.

Phoenyx looked down into her lap, hating answering that question. "He died," she said finally. "When I was thirteen."

"How?"

Phoenyx sighed deeply. "A fire. Our house burned down and he was still inside."

New, warm tears threatened her eyes at the thought of it.

"I'm sorry," Lily said sincerely. "That's really terrible. I can't imagine growing up without my dad."

Phoenyx nodded, fighting back the fresh tears and trying to push these thoughts out of her mind.

"Phoenyx," Lily began, "do you think we are going to die in here?" Her voice cracked at the end.

"I don't know," Phoenyx said. "That's what scares me the most is not knowing anything about the future. Although, I guess if we were going to die, I'd rather not know about it beforehand."

Lily nodded.

"No matter what happens..." Phoenyx said, "you and me are in this together. I'm not gonna let them hurt you as long as I can do anything about it." She gripped Lily's hand and tried to smile.

"I won't let them hurt you either," Lily promised, squeezing Phoenyx's hand right back.

It was then that, looking into Lily's glinting green eyes, Phoenyx felt oddly safe. She wasn't happy for how it happened but she was glad that she met Lily. In the short time that she'd known Lily, she was more vulnerable and exposed than she ever allowed anyone to see. She just ugly cried in front of her for God's sake. She was dirty and smelly for not being able to take a shower and, let's face it, there were no hygiene secrets between them anymore as the toilet was right there out in the open. If she was going to be stuck with anyone in here in such ungodly accommodations, she was very grateful that it was someone as nice and funny and unassuming as Lily.

CHAPTER 4

"Daddy! No, Daddy, come back!"

Clank!

Phoenyx jumped awake, ripped out of her dream by the sound of the door opening. Her heart hammered as she confusedly watched the giant bald man and another large man drag two men—in suits no less—toward the empty cell to the left.

The new captives were both about her age and both distinctly good looking. One had taper cut jet black hair and cool blue eyes rimmed by surprisingly dark and full lashes. He had a long face with a rugged looking angular jaw, offset by his youthful boyish skin. He looked somehow familiar. Had she met him somewhere? The other one had slightly longer, very light blond hair parted to one side, with gray eyes that were covered by intellectual style glasses. Unlike Phoenyx's and Lily's arrival to this godforsaken place, the men were conscious—barely—appearing very drunk.

"All right, all right," the black haired one said with a slurred but still sharp English accent. "I-I think I know what's going on here. This is about Caesar's Palace, right? Look, gentlemen, we can work something out."

Ignoring his pointless efforts of negotiation, using a card to unlock the cell, the two men opened the door and heaved the guys into it like they were rag dolls.

"Ach!" the black haired one complained. "That's no way to treat a guest."

Without even a second look, the large men exited the room and locked the door behind them.

Phoenyx and Lily scooted closer to the bar wall dividing the cells.

"Are you guys all right?" Lily asked.

The black haired one propped himself up to lean on one arm while the other rubbed his forehead.

"Oh, look Skylar, we have company," he said, hitting the blonde's shoulder with the back of his hand.

"Sebastian, could you be serious for a minute, please?" the blonde called Skylar said groggily, apparently less intoxicated than his friend.

"What would be the point of that?" the one called Sebastian laughed like he was the life of the party. "I don't remember drinking so much. Where were we before this?"

"That's because we're not drunk, you idiot," Skylar groaned, rubbing circles around his temples. "We've been drugged."

"Here," Phoenyx slipped her hand through the bars and offered them her water bottle. "This will help with the headache."

Skylar took the water bottle and took a big swig. Then he handed it to Sebastian, who finished it.

"Thank you," Skylar said respectfully. "You wouldn't happen to have some pain killers on you, as well?"

She shook her head.

"What are you girls in for?" Sebastian asked, still smiling like a fool.

"Look, I don't know where you think you are, but I can assure you that you're wrong," Phoenyx said.

"So, this isn't the basement of Caesar's Palace?" Sebastian asked. "The Venetian, then?"

Skylar rolled his glossy gray eyes. "I think what the girl is trying to say is that we're not in Vegas at all."

Vegas? Phoenyx and Lily exchanged a glance, sharing the understanding that two more strangers from yet another completely different state were lumped in with them, further proving that their being here together was planned, that they were hand-picked.

"Could you girls enlighten us as to where we are?" Skylar asked.

They both shook their heads.

"We don't know," Lily said.

"Or why we are here," Phoenyx said. "We've been here for two days now without any explanation."

"Two days?" Skylar asked pensively, trying to process this with some obvious difficulty. "You have no idea what these people want with you?"

The girls shook their heads again. Honestly, Phoenyx was even more confused now with their arrival. She contemplated some kind of serial killer or ritualistic sacrifice scenario, but there were men with them now—men who seemingly had nothing in common with them. Not to mention the fact that these men were from yet another state. What serial killer would go through such trouble? Actually, why would anyone, period, go through such trouble? What the hell was going on here?

"Well, now that we're here, the party can start," Sebastian hollered.

Skylar turned to him and slapped him hard across the face. "Will you snap out of it? I understand that the drugs they slipped us are making you more of a jackass than usual, but we are in some deep shit here. You need to get a grip!"

"*You* get a grip." Sebastian snickered.

"Ugh," Skylar sighed. Putting his palm against the side of Sebastian's face, he said, "Take a nap." Sebastian's eyes closed and he crumpled against the wall, unconscious.

Phoenyx and Lily looked at him with stunned expressions.

"How did you do that?" Phoenyx asked.

"I'm somewhat of a hypnotist." Skylar shrugged. "Just one in our bag of tricks. That's actually what we do in Vegas and why my esteemed colleague assumed we were in Caesar's Palace. Casinos don't take lightly to cheaters."

Phoenyx nodded, secretly admitting to herself that it was pretty cool. It explained why they were dressed in such nice suits.

"I assume that neither of you are cheaters?" Skylar asked.

They both shook their heads.

"Right," he said. "My name is Skylar and Sleeping Beauty over here is Sebastian."

"I'm Phoenyx."

"I'm Lily."

"So, I take it from your confusion at Sebastian's mumbling that neither of you are from Las Vegas," Skylar said.

"I'm from Illinois, although technically taken from California," Phoenyx explained. "Lily is from Washington. Just to clarify, neither of us are any kind of wrong-doers; we are just college students."

Skylar shook his head and pursed his lips. "This doesn't make any sense. What would anyone want with a pair of con artists *and* a pair of college girls? The four of us don't have anything in common? At least, not inherently."

"Actually, I wonder...what's your birth date?" Phoenyx asked, following a hunch.

Skylar raised a curious eyebrow. "June sixth, 1997."

Phoenyx heard Lily gasp, but she continued. "And Sebastian's?"

"Well, that's the funny thing—we share the same birthday," Skylar said. "What does that have to do with anything?"

"Lily and I were born on that day too," Phoenyx said. "I don't know what that means but it is *something* we all have in common."

"How strange," Skylar mused. His eyes narrowed in thought as he put his hand over his chin. "You said you've been here for two days. Have they hurt you?"

"No, not at all," Lily said. "A man comes once a day with food and that's it."

He rubbed his chin, then winced and moved his hand to his forehead.

"Whatever they gave us is really doing a number on my head," Skylar said. "I don't mean to be rude but I have to get some sleep. I just can't think like this. Maybe I'll be able to make more sense of all this with a sober mind."

"Sure," Phoenyx said.

"Of course," Lily said.

Skylar managed a courtesy smile and then curled up on his side on the floor.

"I am so much more confused now," Phoenyx whispered to Lily.

"I am, too," Lily whispered. "Honestly, I feel kinda comforted, too, with men here. This room doesn't seem quite as empty anymore. Even though they are a cell away, I just feel safer knowing they are here."

"Maybe," Phoenyx said. "We should try to sleep too. We can all talk more about this in the morning."

Lily nodded. They went back to their sleeping positions, although Phoenyx knew there was no way she'd be able to sleep after this. There was too much to ponder.

* * * *

Phoenyx heard rustling in the corner of the other cell and turned to her left. The handsome buffoon, Sebastian was stirring. Lily and Skylar were both still out. Phoenyx was glad that Lily was finally getting some real sleep. Maybe her dreams took her to a better place. Meanwhile Phoenyx sat against the wall in silence, trying not to think about anything at all. It was better that way, however boring.

Sebastian pulled himself up into a sitting position and looked around. He appeared to suddenly realize his environment and his eyes widened slightly. When he looked at Phoenyx and saw she was awake, she saw a glint of recognition in his eyes. So it wasn't just her—he recognized her too. The look faded and he got up, gingerly tiptoed around his sleeping friend, and sat as close to the other side of the bars as he could, next to her.

"Hello, there," he whispered, his accent still crisp despite his low decibel. His jackass smile was gone.

"How's your head?" Phoenyx asked.

"Wonderful, actually, because I've always been curious about what it feels like to be rufied," he said, for a minute flashing a perfect crooked smile. "Sorry, bad joke."

Phoenyx snickered a laugh, more at his amazing ability to have a sense of humor at a time like this than at what he said.

"My head hurts so bad I can't even hear myself whispering," he said. "So, I hope I don't sound as stupid as I feel."

"Don't worry about it; you set a pretty high bar for yourself earlier," she teased.

He chuckled softly and his head dropped in humility. "Ouch. I really am sorry about that. I have a hard time taking anything too seriously. I'm ready to listen now if you're willing to shine some light on our current predicament."

"All right, let me fill you in," Phoenyx said. "My name is Phoenyx; over there is Lily. Your friend already introduced you two. I am a college student from California, Lily is a college student from Washington, and you two are a couple of con artists from Nevada. We have no clue what any of us are doing here, and the only thing we all have in common is that we were all born on June sixth of 1997. That about covers it."

He frowned bemusedly. "How weird. We all have the same birthday." He thought for a moment. "Have either of you two girls ever been to Vegas, by any chance?"

"I haven't and I seriously doubt Lily has," she answered. "I really don't think this has anything to do with a gambling debt or whatever trouble you two are in."

"I guess that really should have been obvious when those thugs didn't bloody us up before throwing us in here," he said. "It's not like casino owners to lock up cheaters. They just break a few of your bones and throw you out."

"Well, since you're being so honest here and neither of us is going anywhere, what exactly do you guys do in Vegas?" she asked. "What would anyone want to 'bloody you up' for?"

His smile came back. "Well, I don't usually brag about these things, but—like you said—neither of us is going anywhere. We have all sorts of tricks. For the most part, we play out on the streets, scamming tourists with card games and such. Every now and then, we go into the casinos and use our tricks at the tables. Blackjack is my favorite because you're playing just against the house. More money that way, if you do it right."

"You don't feel bad about what you do?" she asked. "Not that I'm judging or anything."

"Hell no." He shrugged. "We aren't taking money from tourists that they weren't expecting to lose gambling anyway. Casinos make so much money off people every day; trust me, they aren't hurting for what we take from them. It's not like we're stealing or robbing people. To them it all appears fair, money rightfully lost. No one feels any worse off for it."

"Can't argue with that logic." She laughed. "How is it that you can even bet in the casinos when you're under age?"

"When you've done this as long as we have, you don't need to be twenty-one," he said. "As long as you don't look like a teenager, or sound like one, and you know how to play people—they don't bother to check."

"So that's what the suits are all about," she said. He really did look older—not because of his looks necessarily, but just because of how he carried himself. He spilled over with raw confidence and the clean cut black suit made him look like a money shark straight off of Wall Street.

"How long *have* you been doing it?" she asked.

He leaned his head back against the wall. "Oh...about five years, I guess."

"Since you were fourteen?"

"Pretty much. Skylar and I grew up in the same crappy foster home. When we were thirteen, we ran away. We were already so close to Vegas and knew we had a certain knack for lying and tricking people, so it was the perfect place. Things were hard at first but it didn't take long for us to learn the rules of the city and find our niche."

"You grew up in a foster home, you say? Here in America?" she asked. "How did you get that accent?"

"Well, I was born in England. When I was seven, my parents moved here. They died in a car accident not long after. I had no other family in England or America, so I went into the foster system. Got stuck in the same home as Skylar."

"Aww, I'm so sorry," she said.

"Don't be; I'm not," he said. "I mean, yeah it sucks that I lost my parents, and that my foster parents were dead beat druggies, but I'm not sad that I grew up with Skylar. He's my brother, my best friend in the world, and I wouldn't change anything." He said that with such heart, his deep blue eyes sincere as he looked at her. It was so refreshing to find someone with such a realistic, no bullshit outlook on life. Most people with even half as unfortunate of circumstances fed their misery rather than rising above it.

"My, uh, my dad died, too—when I was thirteen," she said, feeling like she needed to share something with him in exchange for all he'd shared with her. "Our house burnt down and he didn't make it out. It's just been me and my mom ever since."

"I'm sorry," he said. "At least you have your mom." He smiled supportively. "I can't imagine how different my life would be if one of my parents survived the crash. I suppose it would have been nice to grow up with a real parent, but that would mean I would have never met Skylar. I don't think that's a trade I would make if I had the choice."

"You guys must have been through a lot together," Phoenyx said.

"We sure have." He nodded. "Poor Skylar never even knew his parents; he'd been in that foster home all his life. The fact that we share the same birthday is actually one of the reasons we got to be so close, I think. Of course, our foster parents didn't give a damn about birthdays, so every year Skylar and I would sneak a little something for each other—that way neither of us had to go without a birthday. Not to mention every other kid in the home was bigger and meaner, so Skylar was really the only friend I had. He still is."

She smiled. "It must be nice to have such a good friend. I had friends back home but none I consider my best friend. After my dad died, we moved from Arizona to Illinois and I had to start fresh. I guess I just never really opened up to anyone enough."

"Well, let's change that right now," he said.

She scrunched her eyebrows at him dubiously. "Right here? Right now? Yeah, I'm so sure I'm gonna make some awesome friends while being held against my will in a creepy prison cell." Never mind the fact that she was already good friends with Lily.

"Sure," he said encouragingly. "Why not make one more friend? You don't have anything better to do. Open up to me, a perfect stranger, and maybe that will help you break your habit. I've told you things I don't usually tell people I have just met. Tell me something about yourself you never told any of your friends back home."

"All right, fine." She snorted a laugh. "Let's see...oh, here's something...I am absolutely terrified of water."

He raised an eyebrow at her and looked as though he wanted to laugh. "Water? Like, *any* water?"

"I mean, like, bodies of water," she clarified. "Lakes, ponds, swimming pools. I can't even take a bubble bath, only showers."

He laughed a little too loudly, causing Lily to stir. He covered his mouth then brought his voice back down to a whisper.

"You're messing with me. Seriously?"

She shrugged and nodded.

"Why?" he asked. "Are you afraid you're going to drown?"

"No, I just innately do not like the idea of being surrounded by water. I don't know what it is."

"So, you've never been swimming before?" he asked.

"Nope. My dad tried to teach me once and I accidently kicked him in the face, trying to get out of the pool. No one ever tried again."

He covered his mouth and laughed as softly as he could manage.

"Wow. I can't imagine never swimming," he said. "I love swimming. Back when I was in school, I was on the swim team; the youngest guy to make it on the swim team in fact. That was the only thing I missed once we ran away. Even now, I can't go one week without having a good swim. You are selling yourself short by avoiding bubble baths. One of life's simplest pleasures."

She shrugged. "If you say so."

He chuckled once and shook his head. "What about this: make me a promise right now that when we get out of here, you will go into a hot tub with me. It's smaller than a pool and shallow enough that you can just sit in it. You don't even have to go all the way in—you can just stick your feet in."

Mildly impressed by his bravado and, for the first time, oddly comforted by the fact that she had no idea if, or when, they would get out of here, she said, "Sure. Why not?"

"You have to say it," he insisted.

She rolled her eyes. "Fine. If we get out of here, I will let you drag me into a hot tub."

"Excellent," he said. "Sebastian Reid, changing lives one hot tub at a time."

She laughed. "You just want to see me in a bikini."

"No," he said sincerely. He then smiled flirtatiously and said, "Not that that isn't a bonus."

Her smile was patronizing but she felt her cheeks reddening with blush. Being stuck here might not be so bad after all.

She changed the subject and they kept talking. It was strange how comfortable the conversation felt, having only just met him. She could talk to him as casually and as easily as if they were old friends. It was never this easy for her. He was so goofy and carefree, which made it even easier. It could just be because they were trapped in this room with nothing better to do. When you're lumped in a life-changing situation with someone, you're bound to feel closer to them by default, right? They talked for a long time, hours maybe, until her lack of sleep caught up to her and she nodded off against the bars.

"I'll let you sleep now," Sebastian said softly.

She nodded again, stopped fighting it, and let her eyes close, welcoming better dreams than the one she'd started this night out with.

It was such a beautiful day to be stuck working in the bar but she didn't hate it. The Mulligan was the hottest bar in town, and only the wealthy came to dance here. The building itself had such an extravagant charm to it. The floor was covered in shimmering white marble—a milky sea with the finest red velvet lounges floating on top here and there. The bar was smooth, rich mahogany, with *artistic carvings climbing all the way up. Behind the bar was a mirror that reached to the ceiling, flanked by bunched red velvet curtains on either side and crowned with upside-down carved mahogany peaks, like teeth pointing down at the bar top.*

The appearance was alluring enough to draw people in, and the music was the reason people stayed. This was the 'it' place for young people. Guys came to show off to their girls, married men came to show off their wives, and single gals came to show off to everyone. Married, dating, or single, the male costumers were always putty in her hands, so their tips made for a great living; getting free drinks every night wasn't half bad either.

She came to work with her hair dolled up like one of the fancy rich ladies, wearing a dress of sequins and sheer, because rumors were going around that some of Al Capone's men were in town, meaning she had the potential to make big money if she played her cards right.

The afternoon was going like any other. All the typical characters brought in a different girl than the night before. Thank God she wasn't as foolish as these girls. She would never fall for any of the crap these sweet-talkers spew, and boy did they ever spew it at her, all the time.

"Scarlett," Mickey, the other bartender called, then slid a shot glass down the bar toward her. She caught it and looked at the brown liquid inside it, the heady fumes of whiskey opening her nostrils. Mickey nodded his head toward a man at the other end of the bar who smiled at her and raised his own glass.

The man was devilishly handsome with jet black hair, the bluest of blue eyes, and a jaw so angular it could cut glass. Judging by the suit he wore, he was no Gatsby wannabe. Something about him was familiar. Had she seen him before? No, she would remember.

She nodded at him with a smile, then took the shot. How did he know that whiskey was her favorite? She walked over to him and decided to chat him up, see if she couldn't flirt a few bucks out of him, or another drink.

"Thank you for the drink," she said.

He nodded. "Perhaps you could tell me your name in return."

"Scarlett," she said. "What's yours?"

"Darian," he said. "Pleasure to meet a real woman in this town."

"A real woman?" she asked, putting her hands on her hips. "What does that mean?"

"You drink whiskey," he said admiringly. "Every other girl in here is drinking a cocktail. You can tell a lot about a girl by the kind of drink she prefers."

"Oh please, do tell," she invited, amused.

"Well, a cocktail says that a girl just wants to be taken care of, and she doesn't like to get her hands dirty. A martini says that a girl will do anything for appearances, because seriously, who actually enjoys the taste of a martini?" She laughed at that. "A gin and tonic says that a girl is dry and boring and sometimes a little bitter. But a whiskey, like a scotch, says that a girl isn't afraid of anything, that she enjoys the simple things in life, and she isn't afraid to take care of business."

"I see," she said, smiling with humor. "So you actually like independent women?"

"Absolutely," he said. "I'll take a woman I can have an actual conversation with any day over arm candy."

"How did you know I drink whiskey?" she asked.

"I didn't," he said. "It was a test of character and you passed. Therefore, I must ask you to dance."

She had to admit, this was already the most interesting and entertaining conversation she ever had with a customer here before. The only things men usually talked to her about were how beautiful she was, or what Wall Street was doing—and oh, she couldn't possibly understand any of it so they will explain it to her as simply as possible—or how much they hate their wives and no one would ever know if she spent the night with one of them.

"All right, I'll dance with you," she said. She stepped out from behind the bar, gave him her hand, and let him lead her to the floor, where they danced to a jazzy new swing song the band was playing.

The scene of the dream changed.

They were in her bed in her small apartment, naked and covered by her satin sheets, heads propped up on bent arms and facing each other. The window was open, a breeze caused her sheer curtains to lift and waft, and silvery moonlight poured in.

They lived together for months. Darian left the mob and worked at the bar as the new piano player. They were together all the time, dancing and drinking during breaks, staying late to clean the bar together because they kept stopping to kiss or tease each other. She couldn't remember a time when she was so happy. Life was perfect.

"There's something I want to ask you," he said. "That night we met in the bar, I just knew you were someone special. I want every night to be just like this for the rest of my life. Will you marry me?"

Her heart leapt. "Yes! Darian, yes!" she exclaimed, throwing her arms around him.

"As soon as I get the money, I'll buy you the ring you deserve," he said.

"I don't need a ring, I just need you." She kissed him.

Suddenly, there was loud banging on the door. Scarlett and Darian turned towards the sound, startled and wondering who banged so fervently. They slipped out of bed and quickly put on enough clothes to cover themselves, then Darian went to answer the door. Before he was halfway there, a gun shot went off and blew a large hole where the handle used to be.

Darian stumble-ran backwards to the other side of the bed where Scarlett was and grabbed her.

"Come on, we have to go!" he said, pulling her toward the open window.

They climbed down the fire escape before the intruders could kick open the door to find them.

The scene changed once more.

She stood in a tiny church, wearing a simple white lace dress. She saw everything through a patterned, white lace veil. Darian, dressed in a snazzy tuxedo, stood across from her, a mixture of happiness and anxiety on his face. She was anxious too. They didn't have very long to stay here. They had been on the run for a long time and, though they wished for this occasion to be grander and for their family members to be present, neither of them could be happier that they were finally going to be wed. Eloping was better than nothing at all, and they didn't want to wait anymore.

"Dearly beloved," the elderly priest began, "we are here today to join this man and this woman in holy matrimony..."

The priest went on with the sermon as Scarlett and Darian stared at each other lovingly, both of them bouncing on the balls of their feet.

"Do you, Darian, take Scarlett to be your lawfully wedded wife, to have and to hold, for richer, for poorer, in sickness and in health, as long as you both shall live?" the priest asked Darian.

"*I do,*" *he vowed.*

"*Do you, Scarlett, take Darian to be your lawfully wedded husband, to have and to hold, for richer, for poorer, in sickness and in health, as long as you both shall live?*" *the priest asked Scarlett.*

She smiled and said, "*No, not only as long as we live but forever after that too.*"

Darian chuckled. Even through the veil she saw tears in his eyes.

"*I now pronounce you man and wife,*" *the priest said.* "*You may kiss the bride.*"

Darian pulled her close, threw off the veil, and kissed her not at all chastely, causing the priest to clear his throat loudly and turn away. Then they ran out down the aisle and out the door, hand in hand.

****

Phoenyx opened her eyes, the dream still fresh in her mind.

What an incredibly weird dream to have right now. She had a different name in it; so had Sebastian. She felt very shocked and slightly embarrassed by the fact that she had such an intimate and girly dream about him after having only just met him. Was she really that attracted to him? Enough to dream about marrying him?

She reflected back on everything that happened in the dream. It was a fun dream, despite its weirdness. She always loved the 1920's—at least she assumed that was the time period the dream was set in. Al Capone, why couldn't he have made an appearance in her dream, rather than just having a mention? She wondered who those people were that had shot through the door. Too bad she couldn't have kept dreaming to find out. Being entertained by her dreams was the only way she would get through this experience.

She peaked over at Sebastian, who was lying against the wall not too far from her. She got an inkling just then, like a sense of *déjà vu*. She had that dream before, hadn't she. That was why Sebastian looked so familiar to her...

No, that couldn't be right. Yes, she'd had parts of that dream before but the guy probably only looked like Sebastian now because she stayed up most of the night talking to him. Yeah, that was more likely. There's no way she could have dreamt about Sebastian before meeting him. Things like that don't happen in real life. Then again, things like someone having the ability she has don't happen in real life either.

She shook her head, leaned back against the wall, and closed her eyes, hoping to get a bit more sleep out of what was left of the night before the others all woke up.

The sound of voices in discussion slowly brought Phoenyx out of slumber. Her face was pressed against the bars and she was fairly certain she had unattractive red lines in their place. She rubbed her eyes and sat up. Skylar, Sebastian, and Lily were talking.

"Morning, sunshine," Sebastian greeted.

She blushed at the sight of him, then quickly got angry at herself for it and pushed those girly feelings aside.

Before she could say anything, her stomach growled loudly, making it known to everyone that she was very hungry.

"Sorry," she said. "This feeding us once a day crap is really not working for me. On the bright side, I'll finally lose those five pounds I promised to lose since Christmas."

Lily laughed. "How do you do that?" she asked. "You just have a way of making every terrible thing seem not so bad."

Phoenyx shrugged. "I don't know, force of habit, I guess."

"Well, I really appreciate it." Lily smiled and Phoenyx smiled back.

"So, what were you guys talking about?" Phoenyx asked.

"Just trying to find a connection we all have," Skylar said. "We really aren't linked in any way. Do either of you have any enemies?"

Lily shook her head and Phoenyx said, "Not that I know of."

"You don't owe anyone money? Maybe your parents do?" Skylar pressed.

"Well, maybe the university," Lily answered. "But I don't think that counts."

"I'm sure we have credit card debt but not in any copious amounts," Phoenyx replied.

"Maybe we're being *Punk'd*," Sebastian said, causing Skylar to sigh and roll his eyes.

"No way! That's exactly what I said our first day in here," Phoenyx said excitedly.

Sebastian laughed.

"Hey, what do you know, Sebastian?" Skylar said, "A girl who actually gets you. Better keep this one locked up."

Sebastian smirked. "My God, Skylar, was that actually a joke?"

Skylar laughed a short laugh. "Anyway, what on Earth could we possibly all have in common? What is the link?"

Suddenly, Lily rushed to the toilet and threw up, stopping all conversation and forcing everyone's eyes to her. She was very pale and her hands were shaking on the rim of the toilet seat.

"Oh, my God, are you okay?" Phoenyx asked fretfully.

Lily coughed a few times and spat into the toilet before wiping her mouth. "I'm sorry. I think I'm just freaking out a little bit." Her voice was weak and wavering.

Phoenyx was really getting worried about Lily. They hadn't had much food the three days they've been in here, and Lily just threw up all the food she did have. If they don't start getting more food, or if Lily couldn't find some way to relax and keep further food down, being trapped in here won't be the only thing they'll have to worry about. Her health could quickly and easily drop in these conditions.

As if on cue, the door opened and the bald man tossed two bags into the room before closing it again. For just a brief second, she noticed a large ring on the middle finger of the hand he tossed the bag with. The emblem on the ring was the exact same design she saw on the pin that guy at the bar wore, the square with the different colored boxes in each corner. Well, in case there was any doubt in her mind that he was involved, she was sure now. Whatever they were doing in this cell had something to do with that symbol.

She crawled forward and pulled the bags through the bars. She took a water bottle out of one and crawled over to Lily.

"Here, you need to drink some of this, sweetie," she said.

Lily sat down and took the bottle with her trembling hands.

Unable to bear seeing Lily so tightly wound, Phoenyx did the only thing that was in her power to do. She put her hand on Lily's arm and, as gently as she could, let her will flow through her hand as she said, "Everything is going to be fine. You're going to drink that water and feel so much better. That burger is going to taste *so* good."

Almost instantly, color came back to Lily's face—her cheeks became beautifully rosy again and the tension in her posture released.

"Okay," Lily said. She took a sip of the water, then chugged it. When the bottle was empty, she said, "You were right; I feel much better."

Sebastian grabbed their doggy bag but Skylar kept staring at Phoenyx, narrowing his eyes in thoughtful scrutiny.

"What?" Phoenyx asked, feeling awkward under his gaze.

As if caught off-guard, Skylar blinked and slightly shook his head. "Nothing," he said and turned to take his share of the bag from Sebastian.

They ate in silence—all of them, or at least Phoenyx, very hungry. Lily was eating her burger just fine. That made Phoenyx so relieved. That didn't mean she could relax just yet; she would have to keep an eye on her and make sure Lily stayed healthy. But for how long?

"I think I know what it is we all have in common," Skylar said, catching all of their attention.

"Oh yeah, what's that?" Sebastian asked mid chew, mostly uninterested in anything but his burger.

Skylar put aside his burger and leaned in toward the bars separating them.

"What you just did to Lily, you've been able to do that your whole life—to anyone, haven't you." He said this to Phoenyx as a statement and not a question.

At the mention of her name, Lily turned to Phoenyx with a question in her eyes.

Phoenyx's heart thudded in her chest.

"What are you talking about?" she asked, trying to keep her voice steady.

"It's okay," he said. "I'm not judging you or accusing you of anything. You don't have to be defensive about your gift."

It was perfectly clear that Skylar knew exactly what she could do. Oh God, she felt like such a freak!

"H-how do you know?" she stuttered.

Hearing the fret in Phoenyx's voice drew Sebastian's attention away from his burger and to both the girls. Now she had everyone's eyes on her.

"Because," Skylar said. "I have a gift too."

Just then, the empty water bottle on the floor to Skylar's right lifted into the air by itself. Phoenyx held her breath and her eyes widened at the sight.

"Skylar, what are you doing?" Sebastian burst out, and he smacked the bottle, causing Skylar to lose his hold over it and sending it crashing to the floor.

"It's all right," Skylar said calmly to Sebastian. "They are just like us. They, too, have secrets."

Phoenyx was paralyzed, trying to process what she just saw and what they were saying. Her eyes weren't playing tricks on her when she saw that bottle levitate. Her hunger wasn't making her delusional. Skylar somehow made that bottle move—with his *mind.*

They are just like us. They, too, have secrets. What did that mean? Does Sebastian have some kind of freaky ability, too? Does Lily? How did Skylar know about me? How could he know I compelled Lily to feel better?

"I'm also a telepath," Skylar said to both girls. "I hear everything you're both thinking."

Phoenyx felt all of her self-conscious blood drain from her face. *He can hear everything I'm thinking? Wait, prove it. What number am I thinking of right now? Nine.*

"Nine," he said, pointing to Phoenyx. "And purple," he said, pointing to Lily.

Phoenyx and Lily gasped in sync.

Phoenyx felt incredibly self-aware now. It was true. Skylar really could read her mind. Every thought she had would not be private as long as she was in this cell with him next door. Her mind might as well be a damn television screen! She felt completely naked.

"Wait, so you're telling me that both of them have some kind of gift?" Sebastian asked. "What's hers?" He nodded to Phoenyx.

She felt like she was on display.

"Yeah," Lily said, still obviously self-conscious herself. "What did you mean when you said, 'what you did to Lily'? What did she do?"

Rather than let Skylar answer and leave Lily feeling violated somehow, Phoenyx figured she might as well explain.

"I can make people do, feel, or say things just by touching them," she confessed, squinting as if the words were physically hard to get out. She turned to

Lily. "I couldn't bear to see you so panicked and you can't afford to throw up with how little they're feeding us, so I *made* you feel better. I had to."

Lily half-pouted and half-smiled. "I thought I felt something...odd. Odd but in a really good way. Thank you. I really needed something to help me calm down."

Phoenyx exhaled and smiled, so relieved that Lily didn't hate her or fear her for what she could do.

"Interesting," Sebastian said, looking smug. "Do it to me. Make me do something."

She raised an eyebrow at him. "Really?"

"Yeah, yeah, come on." He was smiling away.

She hesitated as several slightly humiliating possibilities passed through her mind.

"Yeah, go ahead, make him do something," Skylar said, amused.

Phoenyx could tell he liked what he saw in her thoughts.

Thinking of something she would rather make Sebastian do, she said, "All right," and stuck her hand through the bars. "Give me your hand, Sebastian."

He eagerly came over and put his hand in hers. At the same time Skylar backed away and said, "No, no—not that!"

Putting an extra sensual vibe to it, she pushed her will and said, "Sebastian, I would really like it...if you would give Skylar a big, fat kiss."

Warm color spread over Sebastian's face and he said happily, "Okay!" Then he turned in Skylar's direction, grabbed his face despite Skylar's protestation and hand smacking, and pulled him to plant one right on Skylar's mouth.

Skylar forcefully shoved Sebastian away, then glared daggers at Phoenyx, whose raucous laughter was chorused by Lily's.

"Not cool," Skylar shouted, aggressively pointing his index finger at her.

Sebastian eagerly smiled at Phoenyx.

"That was amazing," he said in a kid's-first-time-to-Disneyland sort of way. "Oddly enough, I have never felt more turned on."

Skylar made a very disgusted face and a guttural gagging sound.

"Oh, don't flatter yourself," Sebastian said to Skylar. Then to Phoenyx he said, "I mean, from your touch, I felt...totally *enamored*, I guess would be the right word for it. In that moment, I was completely willing to do anything you asked."

"Actually, I felt oddly turned on also, despite the icky stomach pain," Lily admitted. "For a moment I almost thought I was going lesbian."

Phoenyx laughed, feeling much more comfortable now. "I don't know why it is but there's always a sensual sort of feel to it. When doing it, I feel this very carnal feeling it in my gut. I think that somehow gets transferred to the person I'm compelling. I really don't get how it works, but it does."

"I bet you're *amazing* in bed," Sebastian said dazedly. Then his eyes widened and his smile fell. He said, "Did I just say that out loud?"

The other three all laughed. Skylar joined in, albeit begrudgingly.

"So, Sebastian..." Phoenyx began, purposefully not addressing his comment and trying like hell to keep thoughts of her dream out of her mind where Skylar could see them, "Skylar said you both have secrets too. What's your special talent?"

"You mean aside from making a fool of himself?" Skylar teased.

Sebastian playfully glanced sideways at Skylar, then said, "I am a master of illusion."

"What does that mean?" she asked.

"I can make anyone see whatever I want them to see," he replied. "For instance..."

Suddenly, barking came from the other side of the bars and, to their amazement, Phoenyx and Lily turned to see an adorable yellow Labrador puppy sitting in front of the door, barking and wagging his tail. Phoenyx, mouth agape, stepped closer, staring at the very real dog in front of her. Then right before her eyes, the puppy disappeared like an image reflected on water whose surface had been disturbed.

"Wow!" Lily gasped. "That was amazing!"

"Thank you," Sebastian said and gave an overly dramatic bow.

"So, this is why the two of you do what you do," Phoenyx said. "You make your money by using your powers and no one is the wiser."

"Exactly," Sebastian said. "It all works out quite brilliantly. Except for in the case when my illusion doesn't reach the cameras in casinos and the owners start wondering why I'm making money off a losing hand. That's the only time we ever get in trouble. I haven't quite figured out how to make more than two or three people see the illusion. Of course, cameras don't pick them up, either."

"That's really very cool," Phoenyx praised. "I think I'd probably be doing the same thing if I had a gift like that."

He smiled and nodded.

"Now then," he said, "that leaves Lily. What can you do?"

Lily froze up when everyone looked at her.

"Why don't you demonstrate on me," Skylar said to Lily. "I have a small Swiss army knife." He pulled it out of his jacket pocket and extended his arm through the bars.

Why would she need a pocket knife? What kind of ability would call for such a tool?

"Really?" Lily asked hesitantly.

"Absolutely," Skylar said confidently. "In fact, I'll make it easy for you." With his other hand, in one swift motion, he opened the pocket knife and sliced a three inch long gash on the inside of his arm. Blood streamed from the wound and dripped onto the cement floor.

"Skylar," Sebastian exclaimed.

"Come on, Lily, there's no going back now," Skylar invited, the epitome of calm.

Lily rushed to the bars and put both of her hands over the bleeding wound. As they all watched with horrified eyes, the separated flesh pulled itself back together and sealed seamlessly. All that remained as evidence of the incident was the blood on Skylar's arm and the few drops on the floor. Otherwise, his arm was unblemished.

"Holy shit," Sebastian exclaimed. "While I have to admit that was a brilliant parlor trick, don't you ever do anything like that again. You scared the bloody hell out of me!"

"Lily, that was incredible!" Phoenyx said, awe-struck. "You can *heal* people. I think you've got the most amazing gift out of all of us."

"Thanks," Lily said bashfully.

"Thanks for not letting me bleed to death." Skylar winked at her.

She laughed nervously. She really was adorable.

He smiled at her. Then he sat down with his legs crossed, all business again. "All right, now that we have all the cards on the table, let's have a real talk."

They all sat in a little circle divided by the bars.

"Now, we know for absolute certain that we were all brought here for a reason," Skylar began. "All four of us have unique gifts. I am a telepath and telekinetic, Sebastian can cause hallucinations, Phoenyx can manipulate will, and Lily can heal wounds. There is absolutely no way this arrangement could have happened by chance. Even so, what could our abilities have to do with us being abducted? What possible motive could there be?"

"Maybe someone wants us to rob banks," Sebastian said. "I wouldn't be against that."

"If something like that were the case, they wouldn't have us locked up in here for days without any communication," Skylar said.

"All right, then maybe this is some kind of X-Men test," Sebastian said.

"X-Men?" Phoenyx asked, one brow raised.

"Yeah, you know, some group like the X-Men could be out there hunting down people with powers and they test them first to see if they are worthy enough to join or something like that," Sebastian explained.

"I think you've read a little too many comic books, my brother," Skylar said dismissively.

"Whatever. Bank robbing, supernatural crime fighting group, I'll take it either way," Sebastian mumbled to himself.

The four of them sat in silent deliberation for a moment. Phoenyx was still reeling over the fact that she wasn't the only freak in this freak show. They all had amazing powers. They were all like super heroes. Although she felt her little trick was far less impressive than any of the others. How did whoever kidnapped them and brought them here even find out about their powers?

"Now that is a really good question," Skylar said to her, making Phoenyx frown at her lack of mental privacy. "There isn't a soul alive who knows about me aside from Sebastian, and vice versa. It's not like either of our talents are obvious in any way. No one can tell if I'm reading their mind and I never use my telekinesis in public. No one can tell that an illusion Sebastian creates is fake. What about you girls? Does anyone know about your gifts?"

"Nope," Lily said. "I've never told or shown anyone."

"No one knows about me either," Phoenyx said. Well, she suspected her father had known but he was dead. "The guy I'm pretty sure is the one who brought me here knew something about it. He could tell I did something strange to the bartender to make her serve me without ID. It was almost like he was looking for it, now that I think about it. How could he have known?"

Skylar rubbed his chin with his index finger and thumb.

"Well, I don't know about you guys but I don't want to stick around here to find out," Sebastian said.

"Let's use our powers to get out of here."

Skylar turned and looked at Sebastian, dumbfounded. "Since when do you have good ideas?" Then they both laughed and Skylar clapped his hands with a newfound eagerness.

"You said someone comes in here once a day to bring food, correct?" he asked Phoenyx.

"Yeah, once a day at random times," she answered.

"So we know that guy will come back tomorrow," he continued. "We will be ready for him. We can use our abilities to make him let us out."

"How are we going to do that?" Lily asked.

"Is your mind strong enough to bend the bars?" Phoenyx asked, half-joking.

"Ha ha, although I've never tried, I sincerely doubt it," he said. "It was actually *your* ability I was thinking of."

She cocked her head in silent question.

"You can get a hold of the guy and make him unlock the door," he explained.

"He never walks in past the doorframe. He just stops right there at the door and throws food inside."

"Then we'll make it so he has to come close. Sebastian, you can make him see something that will lure him close enough to the cell door so Phoenyx can grab his arm."

"What should I make him see?" Sebastian asked. "What illusion would make him come to the cells rather than running off to alert someone? I could give him the illusion of the cells being empty but that would just send him running off in search of us."

"Good point," Skylar said, then frowned in consideration.

"I have an idea," Lily said. "As Phoenyx pointed out to me a few days ago, it's pretty clear they want us alive, for whatever reason. If you made the guy think we were all dead, he would most likely come close to investigate."

"That's brilliant,," Phoenyx said. "It would have to look like we were really clearly dead, not mistakable with being passed out."

"Oh, trust me, I can make us all look very dead," Sebastian said with a wicked smile. "Just imagine a scene from a slasher movie. Blood and guts, that sort of thing."

"Awesome, but what do we do after getting out of this room?" Phoenyx asked. "We have no idea what's beyond that door. They could have guns. I can only control people when I'm touching them, basically one at a time, and there could be a whole army of assholes out there guarding this room. Sebastian, how many people can you make see your illusions at once?"

"I don't actually know," he replied. "I've never tried with more than three people at a time."

"Skylar, how strong is your telekinesis? Can you move people, too? I mean, if someone comes after us, can you push them away with your mind?"

"I've only had to do that once," he said, "when Sebastian and I were on the run from some muggers. That was only one guy I moved. I never had to find out if I could defend myself against more than one person with my mind."

"Look, there may be more dangers waiting out there but we have to try," Sebastian said. "Whatever's out there waiting for us, we can cross those bridges when we come to them."

"Sebastian's right," Skylar said. "We have to get out of here."

"Yeah, I don't want to be here long enough to find out what they want with us," Lily agreed.

Phoenyx nodded.

"Besides, the sooner we get out of here, the sooner I get to see you in that bikini, " Sebastian said to Phoenyx with a wink and a smile.

Skylar frowned and said, "I'm sure I don't want to know what that's about."

"Don't worry your pretty little head about it," Sebastian said. "We're getting out of here tomorrow. Now we just have a whole twenty-four hours to get through in the meantime."

"Well, I know how I'm gonna start," Phoenyx said. She sat back, took the apple out of the paper bag and bit slowly into it, savoring the juices. The burger hadn't even begun to satisfy her hunger, so she figured she had better take her time with the apple, give her body at least the illusion it was getting more food.

"Why don't we play some cards," Sebastian suggested. He took a small, tattered old cardboard box from his jacket pocket. "Here, it's much more entertaining to watch you deal." He tossed the box at Skylar.

"That's a great idea, you're two for two today." Skylar laughed, emptying the cards into his hands.

"Yeah, I have those every once in a while," Sebastian said.

Phoenyx watched Skylar eagerly, guessing that Sebastian's comment about how Skylar deals meant he wasn't going to be using his hands much.

Without saying anything, Skylar gave her a knowing sideways glance, a silent message that he heard her thought and that she was not wrong.

The cards lifted out of Skylar's hands, above his head, spreading out as they did so, and dancing playfully around one another like a swarm of dalliant butterflies. Round and round in circles they flew, forming various shapes in the air. It was such a beautiful thing to see. To have telepathy was one thing all by itself, but to use it with such artistry, such a spark of the imagination, it was simply awe inspiring. Beside her, Phoenyx heard Lily softly sigh at the spectacle.

Then the cards gracefully and softly fluttered like falling feathers into a neat pile in Skylar's right palm.

"So, what are we playing?" Skylar asked, his voice snapping both Phoenyx and Lily out of their stupor.

"Strip poker," Sebastian said, jackass smile in full blaze.

The three of them frowned at him.

"Kidding!" He laughed. "Any game requiring guessing or bluffing is out because Skylar will always win, so I say we play blackjack. That way it won't matter that Skylar knows what cards we all have."

Just like that, the cards lifted out of Skylar's palm and dealt themselves, two to each person.

As the cards went on their merry way, Skylar turned to Sebastian and asked, "Has it ever occurred to you that I don't always like being able to hear everyone's thoughts constantly? If I could block you all out and play a regular game like everyone else, I would do so happily."

When he turned back to the cards, Sebastian looked at the girls and shook his head with a frown that said Skylar was just blowing smoke.

Phoenyx smiled. It was nice to see the way they behaved—the bickering, the joking, and laughing. It was like the comic relief to the horror movie of their situation. Sebastian made it all seem like they were just casually hanging out, like their lives weren't in imminent danger.

Everyone picked up their cards. She had a six of diamonds and a four of spades.

"Phoenyx, you're up first," Skylar said. "What'll it be?"

"Hit me," she said.

A card slid from the top of the deck and glided face down right to her.

She took hold of it and said to Sebastian, "Does this ever get old?"

"Nope," he said and they laughed.

She looked at the card. Eight of hearts. That makes eighteen so far. Three away from twenty-one.

"Are you sure you want to do that?" Skylar asked, before she could say it.

"Eh, I'm a risk taker." She shrugged. "Hit me."

Another card glided through the bars and into her hands. Two of diamonds.

"Stay," she said, without a change in her facial expression.

Skylar merely nodded and turned his gaze to Lily.

"Hit me," she said.

She took one look at her card and said, "Aww, bust," then put her cards on the floor.

Skylar smiled indulgently at her and then turned to Sebastian.

"Stay," Sebastian said, his face stoic.

Skylar raised a scrutinizing eyebrow at him for a moment, then turned to his own cards. On their own, the two cards on the floor before him flipped over face up for all to see: a Queen of clubs and a seven of spades.

"Dealer stays at seventeen," he said. "Show your hands."

Phoenyx laid hers face up. "I have twenty."

"Twenty-one," Sebastian said, laying his cards face up to reveal a King of hearts and an Ace of diamonds.

"Sebastian," Skylar chided.

"What?" Sebastian asked in forced innocence.

"What do you *really* have?" Skylar pressed.

"Just what you see, a King of hearts and an Ace of diamonds," Sebastian replied.

Skylar narrowed his eyes at him.

"Ugh, fine," Sebastian scoffed. Suddenly, the faces of the cards washed away in ripples and became a two of clubs and a ten of spades. "How did you know? I concealed my thoughts."

"I've known you for twelve years, I don't need to read your mind to know when you're lying." Skylar laughed. "This round goes to Phoenyx."

She smiled.

"Trying to rob me of my win," Phoenyx said, shaking her head. "That's no fair using your powers like that."

"Well, you know what they say," he said. "All is fair in love and war."

"We're not at war and no one here is in love," she retorted.

"Not yet, darling." He winked.

Even as she rolled her eyes, she couldn't help but swoon inwardly at the way he said "darling" with that perfect British accent of his.

"Did you say that you concealed your thoughts from Skylar?" Lily asked him.

"Yes," he answered.

"How did you do that?" she asked.

"Lots of practice," he answered. "It takes too much focus to keep it that way all the time. It's all about visualization really. Visualize that you are wrapped inside a soundproof bubble. Feel it wrap around you. When you can feel it like it's almost tangible, then your mind is your own—a closed book."

She nodded. "I'll have to try that." She looked at Skylar and blushed. "No offense to you. I just enjoy my privacy."

"Of course," he said. "I will try to ignore as much as I can."

"Thank you," she said.

"When did you first know about your powers?" Phoenyx asked him.

He cocked his head to one side and looked off at nothing. "I think I've always known. As far back as I can remember, I heard the thoughts of everyone around me. It's always been a burden to me, but on the bright side, it did make it easy to learn to speak."

"What about your telekinesis?" Lily asked.

"I don't remember when I became aware of it but it was pretty early too. Although I didn't really start using it until Sebastian and I went into business for ourselves."

"What about you?" Lily turned to Sebastian as Skylar dealt another hand. "Have you always known about your power, too?"

"Oh no," Sebastian said, looking at his cards. "No, I'll never forget the day I discovered my power. It was a cold winter afternoon, not long after my parents died and I was living at that godforsaken foster home. I was walking home from school and some of the bigger, older kids, the bullies, saw me and chased me. I was pretty torn up right about that time. I was alone for the first time in my life and terrified being in a strange town, I had no one to protect me and really thought that getting caught and beaten up by those kids would be the end of my world.

"Well, they chased me into an empty alley, which, as it always does in those situations, led to a dead end. I was completely cornered with no way out. So, as a means of protecting at least my mind, I imagined a giant black dragon standing behind me, putting its wings around me—I was obsessed with dragons back then. I squeezed my eyes shut, ready for a beating, and wished for that dragon with all my might.

"When the bullies caught up to me, they stopped dead in their tracks. I opened my eyes and saw them staring up, open-mouthed, above my head. I didn't know what they could possibly be looking at and what could have them so scared. I turned around and saw nothing. Wishing desperately for them to just go away, I imagined the dragon in my head roaring at them. To my surprise, they all screamed like little girls and turned tail and ran. I think I even saw one of them pee their pants." He laughed. "I realized what must have happened. Somehow, they saw what I wanted them to see. I thought up that dragon and somehow made it real to them. There was no other explanation for their behavior. So I tested it, small things like imagining I was giving someone a five dollar bill instead of a one dollar bill and successfully walking out of a corner store with five dollars' worth of candy. Ever since then, I've used it to full advantage."

"Wow, that's cool," Phoenyx said. "Sounds like it really comes in handy."

"Only for as long as I can imagine," he said. "There have been quite a few times that I lose focus, get distracted, and then get myself into trouble."

"Yes, Sebastian has quite a knack for that," Skylar said. "Only surpassed by his talent for getting *out* of trouble."

"How was it that you two came to know about each other's powers?" Lily asked.

"We were already becoming close friends at the foster home," Sebastian began. "When I came home that night, Skylar came up to me and told me he knew about my gift because he heard me thinking about it. Knowing that I was different, too, gave him the courage to open up to me about his gift. That secret between us made us thick as thieves."

"Literally," Skylar said with a smile.

They all laughed.

"And you?" Sebastian asked Lily. "When did you discover your power to heal?"

"Oh, uh, well," she stammered, clearly surprised at having been invited to share the history of her gift, "when I was twelve, I had a pet canary named Sunshine. I loved that bird. It was the first pet I was ever given, and I fed it and cared for it almost religiously. One day while refilling her water, I left her cage open for a second too long and she got out. She flew circles around the room before crashing into my window and falling dead to the floor. I was completely devastated. I rushed to her and picked her up and held her in my hands. I wanted more than anything for her to come back to life. I felt my desire for it all through my body and my hands. A few seconds later, as if nothing had happened at all, Sunshine shook her head, popped up to stand on my palm and chirped at me. Totally stunned, I cupped her in my hands and rushed back to put her into her cage before anything else could happen.

"Of course, I doubted for a long time that it was me, that I had miraculously brought her back to life. I believed that she just knocked herself out and then snapped out of it, denying the fact that her neck was clearly broken by the crash. Then one day—years later—when I was driving home from school, I hit a dog by accident. I freaked out and pulled over to check on it. Its hips were broken and it couldn't get itself off the street. I picked it up and carried it to the sidewalk. I felt so horrible for harming such a cute little animal, for not being more cautious. I had to find some way to help it. Then I remembered the incident with Sunshine. Feeling a bit foolish but, fully committed to helping the dog, I put my hands over its hips and just tried. I concentrated on wanting to make it well again. Just like with Sunshine, a second later the dog stood up on all fours, shook itself off, and then ran off into the bushes.

"I always knew I wanted to be a nurse but that day I realized I had an amazing gift. I could really help a lot of people, which just made me want to be a nurse even more."

"That's amazing," Phoenyx said reverently to Lily. She really was something special.

Lily shrugged humbly, looking embarrassed.

"How did you know it would work on people, too?" Sebastian asked. "How did you know it wasn't just animals you could heal?"

"I just believed," she said. "I've tried it on a few patients before, when I volunteered in the children's ward before I graduated high school. All it takes is the true desire to make an ailment go away and it works."

"Your desire to help people is very admirable," Skylar said. "In our line of work, all we see is selfishness. There aren't many people out there who put the needs of others above their own."

She blushed and looked down at her lap.

"All right, Phoenyx, now it's your turn," Sebastian said.

"Oh, uh, hit me," Phoenyx said.

He shook his head. "I mean to tell us how you learned about your gift," he clarified with a chuckle.

"Oh, ha, ha. Actually, I think I've always known about mine too. There was no one moment I remember as being the first time I used it. It's always just been kinda second nature to me. I want something from someone; I touch them and ask for it; I get it."

"Sounds like the perfect arrangement," Sebastian said. "I wish I could do that. Wanna trade powers?"

"Sure," she said jokingly.

"So, basically, you're an only child who always got everything she wanted," Skylar summed up. "Aren't those people typically insufferable spoiled brats? How did you manage to escape that trend? You seem pretty well-rounded to me."

"Oh, trust me," Phoenyx said, "I was well on my way to becoming a spoiled brat. Losing your father kinda breaks bad habits."

"Or creates them," Sebastian said. "Exhibit A." He smiled proudly and waved his hand up and down his body in a displaying gesture.

Phoenyx laughed at him and rolled her eyes.

"I used my power to get whatever I wanted when I was growing up," she continued. "I guess I thought I was entitled to it because of what I could do. Once I saw that it couldn't get me what I really wanted...it couldn't save my dad's life, it couldn't bring him back...I don't know, I guess I stopped taking and started earning. I stopped using it for *everything* and only for small things, whereas the bigger things, I tried to get them the old-fashioned way, like everyone else."

Skylar raised his brows and nodded. "Nice to see that people can grow up, rise above their circumstances—both the bad and the good. We just aren't used to seeing that sort of thing. Maybe there's hope for the world yet."

"If you ask me, not much," Phoenyx scoffed. "Look at where we are. The prime example of someone just taking what they want, whatever that is."

"True," Skylar nodded.

The room was silent for a moment as everyone stared off in synchronized dejection.

"Hmm-mm, Lily, it's your turn, right?" Sebastian broke the silence.

"Oh, yes," she said, coming back to herself. She looked at her cards. "Stay. No busting this time." She giggled.

The game continued, the pace changing to one of lightheartedness.

"So, who's missing us while we're gone?" Sebastian asked the group. "Skylar, I already know that nobody is missing you because I'm your only friend." He smiled teasingly at Skylar, whose face said it was pointless to protest and that the statement was mostly true.

"What Sebastian is so eloquently trying to get out of you two ladies is whether or not you have boyfriends back home," Skylar said.

Phoenyx and Lily laughed.

"I'm afraid Nursing School is the only boyfriend I have time for," Lily said.

Sebastian nodded. "Aww, that's too bad. All work and no play, that's no way to live, Lil." He looked at Phoenyx. "And you? Got a boyfriend waiting for you back in Illinois?"

"Nope, no boyfriend," she replied, unable to hide an amused smile. "I had one but I dumped the loser after he ruined my prom night."

"Ah, so you're on the market," he said. "Excellent. I know we have our little hot tub arrangement but, seeing as we're getting out of here tomorrow, how about you let me take you to dinner tomorrow night?"

She burst out a laugh. "You just don't give up, do you?"

"Never," he said proudly. "So, what do you say?"

"I don't know," she said. "You still have yet to answer the question yourself. A good looking guy like you, with that British accent and a talent for deception, I bet you're quite the playboy in Vegas."

"Please don't inflate his ego anymore; his head can't afford to get much bigger." Skylar snorted.

Sebastian sneered playfully at Skylar, then turned back to Phoenyx. "To answer the question, no, I do not currently have a girlfriend. Sure, I may have had a few romantic mishaps..." Skylar cleared his throat loudly. "...but that's just what growing up is all about, right?" Skylar made a snide comment under his breath that Phoenyx didn't hear. "Besides, like you said, I'm a talented, great looking guy with a British accent."

She couldn't help but giggle at how he twisted her words around. They really don't make 'em in a more charming package than Sebastian Reid.

"Oh, for the love of God," Skylar blurted. "Just tell him 'yes' already so we can get on with the game. I mean, really, Sebastian, you have to try to pick up a girl while we're all trapped in a dungeon?"

Everyone but Skylar laughed.

"All right, yes, tomorrow night, it's a date," Phoenyx said, still laughing.

"Woohoo," Sebastian exclaimed.

Tomorrow night. Here's hoping.

Phoenyx was curled up in a ball on the floor, lying on her side and trying to get to sleep. There was too much on her mind and her body was restless. Tomorrow, they would make their grand escape attempt. How could she not be nervous about that? Then, given that they actually made it out, she had the added pressure of a date with Sebastian. Somehow that made her more nervous than the escape prospect. She hadn't expected to like him. Yes, he was gorgeous and adorable and charming as all get out but she didn't easily fall for a guy's charm. It was probably just the dream from the night before that wigged her out. She did marry him in it. The thought of that was bound to make her focus on him too much and read into everything.

Just turn your brain off, Phoenyx, and get to sleep! You need to be sharp and alert for tomorrow. Now stop thinking!

"Skylar, are you awake?" she heard Sebastian whisper.

"Yes, I can't sleep," Skylar whispered back.

"Me, either," Sebastian said. "Can we talk for a moment?"

She heard rustling behind her in their direction, and she inferred that Skylar and Sabastian moved to sit up against the wall.

"Sure, what's on your mind," Skylar asked. "I don't usually have to ask that question, but there's too much going on in my mind tonight for me to see what's going on in yours."

"Do you remember...the girl I used to always dream about?" Sebastian asked.

Now this got Phoenyx's attention.

"Yes," Skylar said. There was a pause and then he asked, "You think...it's her?"

"I don't just think so, I'm absolutely certain it's her," Sebastian said. "When you see a face a few thousand times over nineteen years, you don't easily forget it—especially when it's a face as pretty as hers. Look at my memories and you tell me."

Another pause. Phoenyx's heart fluttered like a horde of butterflies.

"Hmm, I guess she does have the same face," Skylar mused.

"When I first saw her, when they dragged us in and we were both doped out, I guess I must have thought I was hallucinating or dreaming. The whole situation seemed so much like a dream that it felt right she would be there. When I came back to my senses and saw it was really her, in real life...I felt like I got the wind knocked out of me. I just knew I had to talk to her. All I've managed to do is make an ass out of myself in front of her."

"Well, you're always making an ass out of yourself," Skylar teased.

Sebastian chuckled and she heard a thud as if Sebastian gave Skylar a shove.

"What do you think it all means?" Sebastian asked. "I've dreamed of her my whole life, and now we meet, in a dungeon of all places, and she has powers just like we do."

"I don't know," Skylar said. "I guess the only thing that matters is what you think it means. They are your dreams, after all."

Another pause.

"I think it must be fate," Sebastian said. "I knew I loved her before I ever knew she existed, and meeting her hasn't changed that. Phoenyx is everything I dreamt she would be. She's smart and flirty and confident, a hell of a sharp wit and an even sharper tongue. God, if she uses her gift on me one more time, I think I'm going to have a heart attack. She's...perfect. She's the one I've been waiting for."

Holy crap! Holy crap! Holy crap! Her cheeks burned hot and her eyes opened wide. She hoped they couldn't hear her heart thumping, it was so loud.

"What are you going to do about it?" Skylar asked.

"Well, I'm going to get us out of here first," Sebastian said. "Then...I don't know...I'll do everything I can to win her over."

"Well, I think you're already half way there. She laughs at your stupid jokes." Skylar snickered. "I never thought I'd see the day when you actually got serious about something, or someone. I'm actually kinda proud of you."

"I am definitely serious about her," Sebastian said.

"Well, we'd better get some sleep," Skylar said. "We have a big day ahead of us tomorrow."

"Yeah, you're right," Sebastian said. "Thanks for the talk. If I had to keep all that to myself any longer, I'd go nuts."

"Any time."

Phoenyx heard more rustling and then all was silent, save for the hammering of her heart in her chest and the racing of her thoughts in her head.

Sebastian dreamed about her *his whole life!* He really did recognize her that first night when they talked. She couldn't deny it anymore. Before she ever met him, she dreamt about him. They'd gotten married a hundred times in her sleep. How could this be real?

And he *loved her?* That was really going to take some time to process. Aside from her parents, no one ever said they loved her and meant it. Of course, men told her all the time that they loved her but it was only because they were under her influence. The supposed love they felt wasn't real. Sebastian wasn't under her spell, well, disregarding that little stint with making him kiss Skylar earlier. He said he loved her before he knew she existed. That had to be just about the sweetest thing she ever heard. He loved her, even after seeing what she could do. He didn't think she was a freak. Well, that's only because he had powers too. Was he right? Was this fate?

If she wasn't anxious about their date before, she sure as hell was now. What if she screwed things up? Or said or did something stupid?

Ugh, really Phoenyx, get a grip! You've never let a guy get you this worked up before. Besides, he probably wouldn't love you if he really knew you...

That harsh reality made her heart sink. She wasn't as great and wonderful as he thought she was. She had a dark side. She would only end up hurting him if he got too close.

She exhaled loudly and tried to clear her mind. She didn't have time to think about all this right now. She needed sleep so she could be ready for whatever happens tomorrow. She could tackle all that stuff when this is over. Right now, all that mattered was getting to sleep.

Phoenyx was thirteen. She skipped down the sidewalk after school on a warm autumn Wednesday, swinging her lunchbox back and forth gaily, eager to get home and tell her parents about her invitation to Cynthia Masterson's upcoming birthday party on Saturday. Cynthia was one of the more popular girls in the seventh grade, and they recently became friends. Cynthia was an only child and only had her *wealthy father, so she was usually spoiled with everything she wanted. Her parties were always the talk of the school. Getting invited to Cynthia's party meant Phoenyx was making real friends, and not just forcing people to like her.*

She saw her front yard peek out past the large mesquite tree and ran over the sidewalk and up the stairs, through the front door.

"Mama! Mama!" she called out, darting her head quickly all around.

"In here, dear," Her mother's voice came from the kitchen. "What is it?"

Phoenyx dashed into the kitchen.

The tall, slender, middle-aged blond woman was chopping something on the counter, facing away from the kitchen entrance.

"Mama, I got invited to Cynthia Masterson's birthday party on Saturday! Can I please go? Please? It's gonna be a slumber party and I've never been to one before."

"Ah, that sounds like fun," her mother said, turning to smile at her. "We'll talk to your father about it when he gets home and see what he thinks, okay?"

"Ooookayyy," Phoenyx said, stretching out the syllables adolescently.

She went to her room and picked out the clothes and the toys she would bring while she waited for her dad to come home. She was so excited. She had never been to a slumber party; she never had enough girlfriends. Before middle school, most of her friends were boys, and you can't do anything fun and girly with boys. Girls tended not to like her. She discovered a few years ago that it was because boys liked her so much. Like-liked. She always got the most valentines on Valentine's Day. The pretty girls, the popular ones, could be really mean when they didn't get the attention they wanted. So Phoenyx decided that middle school would be different. She wouldn't even talk to any boys. If she ignored them and tried being really nice to the girls, she might make some real friends. It was actually paying off. Who needs stupid boys anyway?

At around seven o'clock, she heard the front door shut. She keenly hopped to her feet and ran out her bedroom door. She found her father in the kitchen, popping open a can of cola.

"Hey kitten, how was school?" he asked as he scratched his tailored brown beard and took a sip of his soda.

"It was great, Daddy!" she said with excitement. "I got invited to a birthday party—a birthday slumber party, and we're gonna paint each other's nails and have pillow fights and everything—just like in the movies."

"That's great, honey." He chuckled fondly. "When and where is this slumber party?"

"Cynthia Masterson's house on Saturday at five p.m.," she replied, almost panting.

Her father's expression fell from one of indulgence to one of restraint.

"Is her father chaperoning the slumber party?" he asked, his tone dry and deflated.

"Yes, and her aunt too," Phoenyx went on in her enthusiastic manner, not quite aware of, or perhaps choosing to ignore, the change in his demeanor.

He pursed his lips and shook his head. "I'm sorry, Phoenyx, but you can't go to that party."

Her excitement caught dead in her throat and she was completely dumbfounded. "But...why?"

He sighed. "It's...complicated. You're just gonna have to sit this one out, kiddo."

She frowned.

"Daddy, you have to let me go," she implored. "This is the first time I've ever been invited to a party like this. If I don't go, Cynthia will think I don't like her, and then she won't like me, and then her friends won't like me. I've been doing all my homework and I never get into trouble at school. Don't I deserve to go?"

"It's not about that, kiddo," he said, invariable.

"Then what is it about?" she asked, almost demanded.

"I don't trust Mister Masterson, and I certainly don't want you spending the night at his house."

She cocked her head back, bemused. Mister Masterson was a really cool dad. He was always super nice to Phoenyx whenever she came over. He treated her like another daughter.

She wanted to go to this party. She couldn't afford to miss it.

"Dad...," she began, reaching out her hand toward his arm.

"No, Phoenyx," he said sternly, jerking his arm away from her. "Dammit, that's the reason for all of this. Don't you get that?"

Her face blanched and she gasped, stunned at both her father's action and his words. He never jerked away from her like that. What did he mean? Did he know about what she could do? Did he know that if she touched him, she would make him let her go to the party?

"You can't always have what you want," he said. "You're not going, and that's final."

She didn't understand any of this. Why was he so mad? It was just an innocent party. Why was it a crime for her to go? Why was he being so mean?

She felt something stirring up in the pit of her stomach, something similar to the way she felt when she influenced people but this time driven by anger. It was an uncomfortable warmth which began in her very core, and quickly spread through her abdomen.

"You can't make me stay here," she said snottily, that warmth making her lose the control she would have normally kept over herself. "I'm going whether you say I can or not."

"No, you're not! Now, go up to your room and stop being such a spoiled brat," he yelled.

That was the first time he yelled at her since she was a little girl. The words "spoiled brat" coming out of his mouth and aimed at her pushed that feeling in the pit of her stomach past the boiling point, and she felt both a sense of shame and of outrage.

At that instant, the stove top spontaneously caught fire, and the flames quickly raced over the counter top behind her father. The smoke detector began to beep and the argument was forgotten.

"Oh, my God," her father gasped, turning around to stare at the flames as they reached up their tongues to lick the ceiling.

Her mother ran into the kitchen. "What is all this commotion—oh my, what happened?"

"Jane, get the fire extinguisher," her father yelled.

Her mother ran out as her father pulled up the sink hose and began to spray at the fire.

Phoenyx stood still in all of this, gawking at the flames, her mind blank as in a trance. This must be a dream. This can't be real. What started the fire? One second the kitchen was fine and pristine and the next it was up in flames.

Her mother ran back into the kitchen, empty-handed.

Tricia Barr

"I-I can't find the fire extinguisher!" she cried frantically.

The water from the sink hose didn't affect the fire in the slightest, and despite it, flames engulfed the cabinets and drawers.

"Ah Hell!" her father cursed, threw down the hose, and swooped up Phoenyx as he ran out of the kitchen.

Smoke filled all the air and stung at Phoenyx's eyes and throat.

Her blank mind filled with fear. Their kitchen was on fire. At the rate it was spreading, soon the whole house would be, and there wasn't anything they could do about it. How could this be happening?

"Jane, get Phoenyx out of here and call 9-1-1," her father instructed her mother. "I'm going to grab what I can. If the fire spreads to my gun rack, we're screwed."

Her mother nodded.

Her father grabbed her mother's face in both hands and kissed her. "I'll see you guys soon." Then he took off down the hall.

Her mother grabbed Phoenyx's hand and they hurried outside. Heat and smoke rushed out the door with them as the cool night air smacked their faces *with a kind of harsh relief. They kept running until they reached the street. Her mother whipped out her cell phone and dialed with fumbling fingers.*

Phoenyx looked back at the house as her mother spoke to the operator. Flames scratched at the legs of the door frame like cat paws, and small glowing embers flitted out into the night like fireflies.

"Come on, Dad; come on, hurry," she whispered her urgent prayer. Why did he have to stay in there? Forget the guns, forget everything, she didn't care about anything they owned, she just wanted him to come out now and be safe.

Several eternal minutes passed and the flames only spread more rapidly all around the house, with no sign of her father. She couldn't wait anymore; she had to get him out!

She bolted across the yard and sprinted up the stairs, only faintly hearing her mother scream after her to come back. She brushed past the flames at the doorframe, emerging unscathed into the living room. Flames danced across the carpet, twisting and tangling around each other like twirling dervishes.

"Dad!" she called out, the taste of smoke filling her mouth and forcing her to cough. "Dad, where are you?"

She ventured into the hall where she last saw him disappear. It was getting really hard to see anything but she pushed on. She looked around the corner, squinting for any sign of movement. Out of the corner of her eye, she noticed the flames right beside her. She turned her head and saw that the very place she was resting her hand was on fire.

Why couldn't she feel it? She literally felt nothing. As she stared, the bright oranges and yellows blazed on over her hand and wrist, as if they were passing right through her, as if she was a ghost they could not touch.

The image and what it might mean triggered an instant cold fear in her stomach, and then immediately after, the fire began to gnaw at her flesh and she felt her skin sizzle.

"Ahhh!" she groaned, ripping her hand off the corner and hugging it against her chest. "Dad, please!" she cried.

Before she could take another step, large rubber-coated arms wrapped around her and picked her up. Elated that her dad had found her, she turned to look at his face but it was not her dad. It was a man she didn't know, a fireman, and he was carrying her out of the house.

"No!" she yelled, struggling to get out of his embrace. "No, I have to find my dad!"

He pulled her, kicking and screaming, back into the street, as other firemen rushed toward the house with fire hoses.

The fireman released her and she was immediately recaptured by the embrace of her mother, who coddled her and wept over the fresh burns on her arm. But Phoenyx didn't care. She kept her eyes glued to the house, praying desperately that her father would emerge any moment.

Suddenly, there was a boom, and then a louder boom, and then the back end of the house exploded, throwing pieces of wood and embers up into the air, only to land angrily on the ground all around.

"No!" Phoenyx moaned. "No! Dad, come back!"

* * * *

"No!" Phoenyx mumbled, the sound of her own voice pulled her out of her dream as she snapped up into a sitting position, swatting at invisible hands that no longer restrained her.

She looked around, reorienting herself for a moment. Lily was sleeping soundly, and Phoenyx was grateful that her restless sleep sounds hadn't disturbed her. There were sweat beads on Lily's forehead, calling attention to Phoenyx's own sweaty body. It was surprisingly hot in this room. In fact, if she didn't know any better, she could swear the bars of their cell were glowing ever so slightly, and radiating waves of heat.

She turned to her left to check on the guys. Sebastian was snoring faintly, a line of drool dripping on one side of his open mouth. How was it possible that even snoring and drooling he was adorable? She moved her gaze to Skylar, whose own gaze was on her. She gasped, surprised to know that he was awake, and that his eyes bore into her, seeing right through her. What had he seen?

"Can't sleep?" she asked, ignoring the elephant in the room.

"No, it's too hot and uncomfortable in here tonight," he said.

"Yeah, you would think they could at least turn on the AC down here," she said. His eyes were still on her, making her push her hair behind her ear self-consciously.

"Sorry," he said, looking away. "I don't mean to pry. Force of habit."

She nodded. "It's okay. You probably can't always help what you see." She swallowed. "So...you saw my dream?"

He nodded. "I'm sorry about what happened to you."

She nodded. "After years of thinking about it, I understand the reason why he didn't want me to go to that party. Obviously, he knew about my power. How could he not? I'd used it on both him and my mother so many times. He had to know I had used it on Mister Masterson too. I couldn't see it at the time but there was something unhealthy about how much Mister Masterson liked me, and my dad knew it. It was all because of the way my power makes people feel. I brought it on myself. That's why my dad didn't trust him. He was afraid that feeling would lead to...something else."

"That's why you stopped using it," Skylar said. "You blame yourself for what happened to your dad. The fire wasn't your fault. Did you ever find out what started the fire?"

"The insurance investigators said that all they could figure was a fuse had blown," she explained. "They couldn't explain why the fire spread so rapidly.

After the explosion caused by the can of gun powder my dad kept, it was hard to tell what really happened.

"Of course I blame myself for what happened. We were yelling and the next thing I know the house is on fire. I was being a rotten spoiled brat; my dad was right and, because of it, God or whoever punished me. That was a lesson I made sure I heeded."

There was that years old nagging fear coiling in her gut like a snake but she shook it off, refusing to let it surface where Skylar could see. That was one skeleton she wanted to keep buried forever and forget completely.

"Anyway, thanks for listening to me," she said. "I haven't talked to anyone about this since it happened. Actually, I avoid it at all costs most of the time. Thank you for not prying. I can't imagine you want to see people's nightmares."

"You're right about that," he said. "Although Sebastian's dreams are quite entertaining sometimes."

"Oh yeah?" She brightened up. "What's he dreaming about right now?"

Skylar looked down at Sebastian. "He's in a field that is basically a giant pizza. The ground is all cheese, there are giant mushroom cottages and trees made out of pepperoni...and he just dived into a marinara sauce lake." Skylar laughed. "Damn, his hunger is making me hungry."

Phoenyx giggled, picturing the scene of Sebastian's delicious sounding dream.

"Well, I'm going to try to go back to sleep," she said. "See if I can't at least dream about getting some food too."

"Good thinking," Skylar said. "Hey, it's not so hot anymore. Isn't that strange?"

Phoenyx thought for a moment and noticed that all the heat had dissipated and the cement was once again exuding cool like the other side of a pillow. Then she lay back down flat against the cement and let the cool soak into her skin as she closed her eyes and begged for sleep to come soon.

"All right, now before we get too ahead of ourselves, does anyone have any kind of fighting experience?" Phoenyx asked.

Lily's watch showed it was early morning and they prepared themselves for when the large man would return, their chance to escape.

"Well, Skylar and I have been in plenty of fights but we're no heavyweight champs, that's for sure,"

Sebastian said. "As long as we are all vigilant with our powers and you girls scratch and kick and punch whenever you have to, I think we will get out of here just fine."

Phoenyx took in a deep breath, and said, "You're right," as she exhaled.

"Quick!" Skylar whispered loudly. "Someone is approaching the door. Ready, Sebastian?"

Sebastian nodded and then his face went blank with concentration.

The door clanked unlocked and then swung open. This time when the large bald man stepped inside, he paused, did a double take of the room and dropped the large paper bags at his feet. His face went sallow and he looked clearly distraught.

"Shit," he muttered. Then he approached the cell to take a closer look and assess his next move.

As soon as he came close enough, Phoenyx grabbed his arm. He jumped in shock and confusion, but then quickly relaxed, soothed by her touch.

"Don't be afraid," she said in a sultry voice. "You want to help us. All you have to do is unlock these cells and let us out."

"I would but I don't have the key," he said, his eyes locked on hers, looking like a love-sick puppy.

There was a collective sigh of disappointment behind her.

"Who does?" she asked.

"Dexter has it," he confessed eagerly.

"Is there any way that you can get the key for us?"

"Uhhh, I don't know," he said. "He keeps it hidden in his office and no one is allowed in there. I will gladly try."

She frowned. *Why did we just assume this automaton would have the key*? This really put a damper on their plans.

"Ask him what we're doing in here," Sebastian whispered.

"Right, why are we locked up in here?" she asked the oaf.

"Because, you four are the Bound Ones, from the legend," he said as if it was simple and obvious.

"The Bound Ones?" she asked, feeling like she just stepped into *The Twilight Zone*. "What legend?"

"Yes, the legend we learn when we join the brotherhood. The legend of the Bound Ones says that, thousands of years ago, man was a slave to the elements. Man could not master crops because Earth was fickle. Volcanic eruptions would swallow whole villages and earthquakes would topple any and all of man's accomplishments. Man could not master the sea because Water was too proud to be tamed. Air constantly tore apart cities with tornados and hurricanes, and Fire ravaged everything in its path. So our forefathers, the wisest of the Celtic sorcerers, forged a powerful spell binding each of the four elements to a volunteer from the rite, so that man would have control over the elements, rather than be controlled by them."

"So...you're saying that the four of us each have one of the four elements inside of us?" she asked, unable to keep the tone of doubt from spewing out.

"Yes, you are Earth, Air, Fire, and Water in bound human form," he said, as if none of this sounded ridiculous.

Phoenyx turned around and looked at the others. Their faces were a mixture of skepticism and pensiveness.

"If this is true, what makes you think *we* are these Bound Ones? Wouldn't they be long dead seeing as this legend happened so long ago?" Skylar asked.

"According to the legend," the bald man began, "the spell was made to keep the elements bound in human form through reincarnation. The elements are eternal and cannot be destroyed, so if the bound human died, the element would once again be free. The spell was made to assure that once the human died, the element would be immediately reborn into another human vessel. Unfortunately for our forefathers, they didn't take into account how that would make it impossible to keep track of them. After the first volunteers died, we lost hold of them permanently."

"That still doesn't explain why you think these Bound Ones are us particular four people," Skylar argued.

"There was another partition in the spell," the man continued. "When one of the Bound Ones dies, all die, and when one is born, all are born."

That struck a chord in all of them.

"That's why we all have the same birthday," Lily said.

"That's why they want to keep us alive," Sebastian said. "They think if one of us dies, we'll all die."

"Yes," the man said.

"That doesn't prove anything," Sebastian said. "So we were all born on the same day. Big deal. There must be thousands of other people all over the world born that same day."

"You were all born, not just on the same day, but at the exact same time," the man said. "Your births coincided with the deaths of four people who showed signs of being the previous Bound Ones."

"We were all born at the same *time*?" Lily thought out loud. "That would definitely bring the odds down quite a bit. Approximately two-hundred and fifty people are born every minute—at least, that's what I remember from my nursery rotation."

This was ridiculous. It had to be. These people clearly had some screws loose...then again, the four of them *did* have powers. That couldn't just be coincidence. That same nagging, writhing feeling reared its ugly head once more. She ignored it and went on with the interrogation.

"Okay, so let's say we are the 'Bound Ones'," Phoenyx said, air-quoting with her free hand. "What do you want with us?"

"The Celtic sorcerers who bound the original humans founded a brotherhood to keep an eye on the elements, to keep everything in balance, and called it the Four Corners." He moved the fingers of his free hand over the pin on his shirt. "Dexter Mauldive, our

Grand Master, convinced the High Council that it was time to put the elements back under our control, and that it would be best to put all four elements into only one vessel, making it easier to relocate them after each rebirth. He has volunteered to be the first."

"Just how do you plan to do this?" Skylar asked.

"We have realized that we can't just kill you, because then the elements would immediately be reborn somewhere else and we would lose them once more. Our best researchers have said that the elements must be in a sort of limbo state in order to be manipulated and placed inside a new host."

Phoenyx swallowed hard. "Limbo state? How will you accomplish that?"

"There is currently a massive solar storm happening. In three days a very rare, very large solar flare is forecasted to explode. Our researchers say the radiation and electro-magnetism this will release will both heighten the powers of all four elements and weaken their hold to your bodies. On that day, the four of you will undergo a series of electrocution which will further weaken that hold enough for the spell to work. In order to break down your bodies even more in preparation for the ritual, we were going to starve you. This is the last time you will be fed."

Phoenyx's heart pounded wildly and the hand she grasped him with was trembling and dripping cold sweat. Holy shit, this was so much worse than anything she could have imagined in her head. The prospect of being killed was already bad enough but to find out that they were going to be starved an electrocuted? This was a goddamn nightmare!

She sensed Lily was crying. Like hell she was going to let this happen to them!

"What's your name?" she asked, her steady voice disguising the panic and anger she felt.

"Lucas," he answered. She noted to herself how creepy it was that, even as he told them about all the horrible things that his cult planned for them, he still gawked at her like a horny gorilla.

"Lucas, you have to bring us that key and get us out of here," she commanded, pushing her will into him with everything she had. "At all costs but be discreet about it. Do you understand?"

"Yes," he said, almost like a moan of pleasure.

She released his arm. "Now go, and hurry!"

He nodded eagerly, moved the last brown paper bags closer to the cells, and left the room.

Now that he was gone, the room was dead silent, except for the loud banging of Phoenyx's heart. No one spoke for a very long moment. Finally a sniffle escaped from Lily. Phoenyx instinctively turned and put her arms around Lily, inviting Lily to stop holding it in and her tears soaked into Phoenyx's already quite dirty shirt. Phoenyx had no words to comfort her with this time. If Lucas didn't come back to free them, they would die.

"This is bullshit," Sebastian said finally. "These people are fucking psychos!"

"That may be," Skylar said. "I saw it in his mind; they all believe it down to their core. They live it and breathe it. The question is, do *we* believe it?"

"Hell no!" Sebastian said. "Who the hell could believe that anyone could actually imprison the elements, like they were actual beings? This isn't ancient Greece; it's 2016 I don't even believe in God but I'll believe in him long before I swallow any of that nonsense."

"I don't know," Skylar said. "It can't just be a coincidence that we all have these powers. It's not every day that four people, born at the exact same time, all have Marvel-esque super powers."

"So, what you're trying to tell me is that you actually believe the four of us are Earth, Air, Fire, and Water? You've been in this damn cell for too long."

That uneasy feeling was growing and scratching at her insides, making her queasy. Lily had stopped crying and listened to them argue. Phoenyx only held her tighter, herself wanting to be held as she felt like she might jump out of her skin.

Skylar, who was about to say something, paused mid-breath and looked at Phoenyx, and she knew what he was thinking. It was the same thing she had kept herself from thinking for six years, the thing she always suspected in the back of her mind but never wanted to face.

"Phoenyx, your dream," he said softly, his brow creasing up in apology and pity. "Oh, I'm so sorry."

The feeling erupted inside her, icy cold fear flooding her veins as if the hand of Jack Frost was squeezing her heart.

"What?" Sebastian asked, wanting to be let in on the secret.

"That's why it was so hot last night," Skylar continued. "You were making it happen and didn't even know it."

Her breaths came faster and faster, without her consent. Jack Frost's hands were closing in around her neck, making it harder to breathe. She could barely hear the fretful voices of those around her as she hyperventilated. Memories from that night flashed in her mind. The fire in the kitchen. The anger she had felt right before. The explosion. The way her hand didn't burn.

"Calm down!" Sebastian urged Phoenyx, as he pressed up against the other side of the bars, reaching out to her.

Lily rubbed her back desperately, then she grabbed one of the empty paper bags and handed it to her.

"Put this over your mouth and breathe into it," Lily instructed. "Try to calm down."

Phoenyx did as she said, panting repeatedly into the bag.

"What's happening?" Sebastian whimpered. "Why is she freaking out? What did you do to her?"

"I'm sorry, Phoenyx," Skylar said, calm and yet pleading at the same time. "I'm sorry but we have to face all our demons if we're going to get out of here."

"What demons?" Sebastian demanded, shoving Skylar's shoulder.

"There is at least some truth to what Lucas said, because compulsion isn't Phoenyx's only power," Skylar explained. "She can also start fires with her mind."

"No!" Phoenyx screamed, throwing down the paper bag, tears streaming down her face. "No, no, no, it can't be true!" She buried her face in her hands, wishing desperately that she could hide from everything.

All this time she blamed herself for her father's death because she knew in her darkest depths that she had started the fire! It never really seemed possible, so it was an easy thing to ignore, to deny, even with her dreaming about it at least once a week for six years. She couldn't deny it anymore. It was all true! They really were the living embodiments of the elements, the Bound Ones. She was Fire and had killed her father. She was a terrible person.

Soon all she heard was her own hiccupping. Jack Frost's hands crept up until they covered her eyes, and the world turned upside down. Then all she knew went black.

"Phoenyx, wake up," a pretty, concerned voice wafted through her unconsciousness. She felt light slaps on her cheeks, and then the blackness dissipated and she was fully conscious again.

She opened her eyes to see three distressful faces looking down on her.

"Are you okay?" Lily asked, pulling Phoenyx up to sit.

"What's going on?" Sebastian asked, his hand

sneaking through the bars to rub her arm.

The blackness had taken none of the pain or the guilt with it and the panic quickly returned.

Tears streamed from her eyes, a dam over-flooded with unrestrainable emotions. "I killed him," she sobbed, her voice cracking and her face wrinkling. "It's all my fault. He was only trying to protect me, to be a good dad and I killed him. I'm a horrible person. It should have been me!"

No one spoke as she broke into a heavier sob. She didn't care to look up at their faces. It didn't matter what opinion her confession wrought in them, because no one could judge her as harshly as she was judging herself. "I never wanted to believe it, but...what Skylar said is true. I can start fires with my mind. Or at least I did once. I..." She half-hiccupped, half-sniffled. "I killed my father!" The sob took over and her shoulders shook.

"Oh, sweetie," Lily crooned, rubbing Phoenyx's back comfortingly.

Phoenyx could hardly feel the touch. She was so deep inside herself, in a place where nothing felt good.

"You didn't kill him," Skylar said. "You may have *unknowingly* started the fire but his death was an accident. You have to know that's true."

"If I hadn't lost control, if I hadn't gotten so angry that the fire sparked, my dad would still be alive!" She wept. "Whether or not I intentionally killed him, it's still my fault he's dead!"

Sebastian reached in further and took her chin in his hand. He gently turned her face toward him.

"Do you really think your dad would blame you?" he asked. "If he's up there somewhere watching down on you, do you think he could actually blame his only daughter for an accident that ended his life?"

"God, I hope not," she cried.

"I'm sure he doesn't," Sebastian said. "You can't beat yourself up about it your whole life. All you can do is learn from this and move on. Don't you think that's what your dad would want for you?"

She nodded. She sucked in through her nose as hard as she could and wiped her eyes. Then the knowledge that all their lives were in imminent danger came back to her. They couldn't afford for her to get caught up in her remorse right now. She had to get it together, for them. She had to bury these feelings, at least until the time came when she could deal with them in private. That was one thing with which she had lots of practice.

"It's okay. I'll be okay," she managed to say convincingly. She swallowed hard, forcing her feelings back down with it. "We have more important things to deal with. Now that we've established that I'm a freak firestarter, that means the legend is true to some extent. They chose right with me, and seeing as you all have powers, too, I'm guessing they weren't wrong about you three, as well. So...which of the elements do you all think you are?"

It was clear on all of their faces that no one wanted to abandon their concern for her, that none of them were convinced she was okay but they did slowly give in to ponder the question she posed.

"Air, Water, and Earth are left," Sebastian mused. "I know it's probably too soon to joke about but I'm a little disappointed that Fire is already taken."

Phoenyx mustered up a fake smile for him. He returned one, and she saw his compassion for her in his eyes. How could he still like her after what he just learned? His affections were completely undeserved.

"Maybe our powers have something to do with which element we are," Sebastian said. "The core of Phoenyx's ability to control people's will is rooted in sensuality, right? Doesn't fire have something to do with sex and sensuality? People always say things like passion burns. Fire is unpredictable and wild, just like lust can be."

"That's a good point," Skylar said. "I think you've got something there. So then, what do our powers say about us?"

"Well, I see a connection right away," Lily said. "With you, Skylar. You are telepathic and telekinetic. Everything about what you can do deals with the air. Thoughts are a frequency, frequencies move through the air. Moving objects with your mind—isn't that manipulating air in order to move things?"

"Wow, that's...an amazing observation," he said with a look of revelation on his face. "I think you're absolutely right."

"Lily's ability to heal," Sebastian said, looking like he just had a eureka moment. "Earth is always referred to as Mother Nature, and isn't Mother Nature supposed to be nurturing and healing?"

"She loves to garden," Phoenyx interjected. "She told me, before you guys were brought in, that she was in the garden club at her school. Didn't you say your nickname was Green Thumb?"

"Actually, I...I do have a knack for growing things," Lily admitted. "My ability to heal isn't limited to people and animals. It works on plants too. I can accelerate their growth. I can make a flower go from a seed to a blossom in minutes."

Of course Lily would be Earth. She was sweet as a garden in spring. She was selfless and loving and friendly, and yet so frail, a flower requiring the utmost care. She was the best of all of them. And Phoenyx believed she was the worst.

She felt Skylar's hand on hers then. She looked up at his face. He shook his head, and his gray eyes were full of sincerity. She appreciated the gesture but it didn't change how she felt. *Thank you*, she thought, and then she did what Sebastian said he did—she visualized a bubble all around herself, so tight and thick, to close her mind off to him. She saw the change in his face, so slight, so subtle, as was everything else about him. He nodded, patted the top of her hand gently, then pulled his hand back through the bars.

"Well then, that leaves Water," Sebastian said. "I'm Water?" The words turned into a question as he spoke them.

"Come to think of it, your illusions have always had a ripple look to them—when they fade anyway," Skylar said. "You've always loved water. You'd swim all day everyday if you could."

"Oh yeah, didn't you tell me you were the

youngest kid on the swim team before you left school?" Phoenyx recounted. "It would make sense if you were Water."

"Sure, I love swimming and playing in water, but that's just the kid in me," Sebastian said with a shrug. "What do illusions have anything to do with water?"

"That's simple," Lily said. "Think about reflections. Water reflects and even changes images."

"Yeah, like mirages," Phoenyx added. "Mirages can make people see all sorts of illusions. Water can be tricky."

"That's definitely Sebastian," Skylar said. "Tricky."

"Water is also adaptive," Phoenyx said. "It's kinda like Bruce Lee's famous saying. 'When you pour water into a cup, it becomes the cup. When you pour water into a bottle, it becomes the bottle.' From what I know of you, whatever situation or environment you are put in, you mold yourself to fit into it and best it."

"She quotes Bruce Lee," Sebastian said, looking at his lap and shaking his head. "Let's say I am Water." He rolled his eyes at the last word. "All three of you can manipulate your supposed element: Phoenyx starts fires, Skylar moves things through thin air, Lily makes plants grow. I have never manipulated water."

"Actually, that's not true," Skylar said, pointing at Sebastian with his index finger. "There have been countless times that I've seen you stay under water for longer than is normal. I think your record is thirty minutes. That must be because you are manipulating the water to stay submerged longer, and you don't even realize you're doing it."

"Thirty minutes?" Lily asked. "He's right. That's not humanly possible. Most people tap out at three minutes, a tenth of your time."

"Really?" Sebastian asked. "I guess I never really thought about it. It's always just been natural to me to stay under that long." He fiddled with his fingers on his lap. "I still think this whole thing is ludicrous. I refuse to believe that thousands of years ago, a band of cracked out wizards trapped the most basic laws of nature in human form. I mean, it's just fucking bonkers. Hell, what's next? Are you going to tell me the Tooth Fairy is real? That unicorns and mermaids exist? That there really is a jolly old fat man named Santa Claus who travels the entire world in one night, delivering presents to good little boys and girls? If that's true, that bastard owes me ten years of presents."

"It doesn't matter if the story is true or not," Skylar said. "The fact is, we do indeed have the powers they say we do, for whatever reason that may be. Regardless of the reality of spells and rituals and ancient spirits, these people are going to kill us. I don't imagine they expect us to walk away from being stripped of these elements."

"Our only hope is that Lucas returns quickly with the key," Phoenyx said. "Before the effect of my compulsion wears off."

"How long does it usually last?" Skylar asked.

"I put every ounce of will and force I had into the order I gave him," she said. Maybe a little too much, for she barely had enough left to compose herself after her harsh realization moments ago. The void of pushing out all her willpower left her vulnerable. What horrible timing!

"Depending on the purpose and the effort I put in, the effect can last anywhere from a few seconds to a few minutes to a few hours. This one will be on the latter end of the spectrum for sure but it's not an exact science. I can't predict a definitive time frame."

"We'll just have to hope it's enough," Skylar said.

CHAPTER 12

"Now I guess we just wait," Sebastian said.

Another long, echoing silent pause began. It was hard to tell anymore how long anything was. Every second filled with silence crept by slower than molasses dripping down a tree on a cold day. Phoenyx couldn't bear this. She couldn't bear the loneliness of the silence. It invited all her horrors to come to the surface, to whisper in her ears terrible truths she didn't want to hear.

"Ugh, I can't stand all this waiting around!" she grunted. "I *hate* just sitting here waiting for someone to come, waiting for our fate to be decided, waiting for food that stopped coming. I hate when everyone is quiet and no one is talking. Most of all, I hate this God forsaken room!"

"We all do," Lily said.

"So, can we please just talk, about anything?" Phoenyx beseeched the others.

"I can do you one better than that," Sebastian said.

Before Phoenyx could ask what he meant, the cement floor on which she sat softened and went from dull gray to bright yellow-brown, turning into sand. The sand spread and radiated from underneath her to cover the entire floor of the room. The iron bars that separated and confined them disappeared slowly from bottom to top. At the center of the ceiling, the cement cracked and crumbled into oblivion, revealing glorious, vibrant blue sky behind it, until all the cement of the ceiling and walls disintegrated and opened up to a lively and spacious beach.

Phoenyx stood and did a three-hundred-and-sixty degree turn, absorbing everything she beheld. No longer were they trapped in a tiny room. She felt the sand crunch beneath her feet. She felt a sea-breeze softly caressing her face and brushing past her hair. She smelled the salt in the air and was so grateful for the warm feeling of the sun shining down on her. She heard laughter behind her and turned to see sprightly bikinied, teenage girls running toward the distant shore with a beach ball.

"Is this real?" Lily asked, picking up a handful of sand and letting it spill between her fingers.

"As real as you believe it is," Sebastian replied.

"Wow, I knew you could make people see things but I never imagined you could do *this*," Phoenyx said, in awe. "I mean, it's not just an illusion; it's not just sight and sound, I can *feel* it. I can't find a single flaw in anything I'm seeing. If I didn't know any better, I really would think I was at the beach. Thank you."

"You're welcome," he said, smiling fondly.

"Can you see your illusions like we can or is it all just in your mind?" she asked.

"I can see it if I choose to," he answered. "Like right now, I'm seeing everything you're seeing as if it were really here. For most of my illusions—when I'm trying to get away with something, for example—it's easier to see what's real."

"If I had your powers, I'd probably put myself somewhere else all the time," she said, staring out at the waves crashing up on the beach's end.

"He used to," Skylar said. "When we were at the foster home, Sebastian would turn our box fort into a grand castle, in which he made us kings. We would fight dragons and rescue damsels. We had quite a wild fantasy life."

"Wow, I used to make believe as a kid too but that would have been so much more fun." Phoenyx laughed. "Now, can you imagine us some ice cold beers? What's the beach without beer?"

Sebastian laughed. "I could try but it wouldn't be as good as the real thing. That's one thing I can't get quite right. Taste. I guess because everything tastes different to everyone. Taste is the only one of the five senses that's relative."

She sat back down and rested back on her hands to look up at the sun. It really did leave greenish-purple spots in her vision. What an amazing trick this all was! She could pretend that the sting in her eyes was from the salty ocean air rather than from days and nights of on-and-off crying. She could even almost ignore the hallow pain of hunger in her stomach and the constant aching of her spine and shoulders and hips that sleeping on the hard concrete produced.

"I think we've all had enough sitting for a while," Sebastian said. "What say we play a game?" He held his hand up, palm open, and a volleyball materialized there. Just as suddenly, a volleyball net manifested right down the middle of the group, where the iron bars had been.

Happily and eagerly, they all stood to play. Sebastian held out the ball with one hand and curled the other into a fist to hit it upward and over the net. They hit it back and forth for a long time, laughing every time someone missed, or every time someone got hit by the ball. It became pointless after a while to keep score. Lily was a terrible aim and missed the ball constantly, which only made her more endearing to the others.

Phoenyx couldn't get over how real it felt. She was absolutely lost in wonderment. That Sebastian could make all this was nothing shy of incredible. She couldn't imagine the sheer amount of focus that *creating a world* must take. To have to pay attention to all the little details, like the way sand looks; how each and every grain is unique with its own shape and glint and color; and all the people around them. There were voices of teenage girls running around and the laughter of the kids building a sand castle further down the beach. All the voices were unique and individual. He must be thinking about it all right now, producing each and every detail with his mind moment by moment, and still socializing with the three of them, playing, and having a good time.

She watched him as he leapt up to hit the ball with the top of his head. He came off so goofy and fun-loving. She understood he had a whole other side to him. It was a secret he hid from everyone, even from himself, that he was really quite brilliant. His nonchalant and devil-may-care attitude was an escape from a mind as busy as a super computer.

The ball came her way. She jumped out of her consideration to hit it back over the fence.

"Ah, I need a breather," Sebastian said after a while. His jacket and white button-down shirt were now off and thrown to the side. She admittedly had trouble paying attention to much else. "Phoenyx, do you wanna take a break with me?"

Dammit, stop staring at his chest. "Sure, I could go for a drink of water right now anyway," she said casually.

He walked around the net and up the beach;

she followed. It was only after they were a noticeable distance away that she realized something was wrong. It wasn't possible that she and Sebastian could walk this far away from Skylar and Lily, the cell they were in was too small for that.

"Sebastian, how is it that we are so far away from them?" she asked as he sat down in the sand. "We shouldn't be allowed to walk more than three steps away from them. The cell is too small for that."

He chuckled softly. "Then you weren't paying much attention. How many steps *did* you take?"

She was about to say that she clearly took several steps, but then she stopped short. She thought about it and realized she had only really taken about three steps. Why did it seem she walked much farther? If she only took three steps, how was she so far away from Lily? She hardly heard Lily from here.

"That's all part of the illusion," he said. "Much of what even the real world *is* is what people perceive it to be. It doesn't always matter what actually is. So, if I make it seem like you've walked much farther away than you actually have, your mind will make up for it by perceiving something to make that more understandable. That's why Lily and Skylar can't hear us right now. They perceive that there are yards between us, when they are actually still only inches from us."

He just gets more and more amazing, doesn't he?

"So, they can't hear us talking right now?" she asked.

"Nope."

"So, Lily is still right next to me?" she asked. "If I stick my hand out right now in her direction, I won't be able to touch her?" She did so without waiting for his answer. She extended her arm as far out to her right as she could, right at Lily, but there was nothing but air. "This is so trippy."

She withdrew her arm and sat down in the sand next to him.

"So, about our date tonight..." he said. "I think we are going to have to reschedule."

For an instant, her heart ached and she felt rejected. She couldn't blame him. He just learned she was dangerous so why would he want her? She kept her cool.

"Chickening out already?" she asked playfully.

"Fat chance," he said.

Relief washed through her.

"Any nice restaurant I would want to take you

to would be filling up right about now."

"How do you figure that?" she asked.

"Because it's seven o'clock," he answered.

She was taken aback. She looked all around. The sun was still in the same place in the sky it had been when they got here, so to speak.

"Have we really been playing all day?" she asked. "I didn't even realize so much time passed. With the sun in the middle of the sky like this, I could play under it for hours more."

He smiled. "I'm glad I could help put a smile back on your face. You had me pretty worried earlier. Do you want to talk about it?"

She looked out at the ocean, her throat tightening, making her unable to speak for the moment.

"You don't have to," he said. "I just wanted to understand. This has been the first time that Skylar's telepathy made me feel left out rather than clued in. I guess I just don't know how to handle it—especially when it concerns someone I'm starting to care about."

The handsome fool wasn't present in the face that was looking at her. His blue eyes ran deep, revealing the profound person inside she was realizing him to be. It felt again as though she had known him forever, like she could tell him anything. Hell, if the legend was true, perhaps they really had known each other forever, in hundreds of other lives.

Then it dawned on her...the dreams. She dreamt about Sebastian and he dreamt about her. They *had* met before. They must have. They weren't just dreams, they were memories. The legend said that the elements were destined to reincarnation. It wasn't just the elements, it was *them*—the souls the elements were bound to—that were also reincarnated. Suddenly, she was no longer afraid of scaring Sebastian off. She knew without a doubt that it just wasn't possible. She could open up to him without fear of rejection.

"I came home from school one day and asked my dad if I could go to this party I was invited to," she said. "He said 'no' and we got in this huge fight and...I don't know...I got so angry. That was a time in my life when I really was a spoiled brat. I knew I could get just about anything. So when he refused to let me go, at a time when making friends meant everything to me, I didn't know how to handle being told 'no'. I always knew that it was me who started that fire. Even though it didn't make any logical sense, I felt it.

"The fire started in the kitchen behind him and spread all over the house so quickly. My mom pulled me out and my dad ran back inside to get something. I ran in after him and got carried out by firemen right before the gun powder supplies caused the explosion that ultimately killed him."

Sebastian put his hand over hers. "That's how you got your scar." They both looked at it then.

"When I ran inside to find my dad, I had my whole arm right on a part of the wall that was on fire and I didn't even realize it," she explained. "I couldn't feel it at all; it was like the fire wasn't even real. When I realized that the fire wasn't hurting me, it scared the hell out of me, and it was only then that the fire started to burn. Because I had my arm so deep in the fire, it took a lot more skin than burns usually do. That was another part of the story I could never explain, until now. That's why it was so easy to deny for so long."

He moved his thumb over the scarred flesh; such a gentle touch sent a shiver across the surface of her arm raising goose bumps.

"It doesn't sound to me that his death was your fault," he said.

"If I hadn't caused the fire, he'd still be alive," she protested.

"No, if he hadn't gone back in, he'd still be alive," Sebastian corrected. "It was his choice to go inside a burning building; he knew the dangers. He just wasn't lucky enough to make it out. It was an accident."

"Just because something is an accident doesn't mean someone isn't guilty for causing it," she argued.

"Just because someone is guilty doesn't mean they deserve to be punished," he countered. "You most certainly don't deserve to punish yourself forever."

"Maybe." She shrugged.

"Besides, you're Fire; for you forever is a long time," he joked.

She scoffed. "I thought you didn't believe in any of it."

He pursed his lips. "I don't...but I remembered something, an incident, from when Skylar and I were kids. It has me thinking. It could have been a coincidence but, if I've learned anything from this whole experience so far, it's that there are no coincidences in life."

His eyes met hers. She could tell he wasn't just talking about their powers.

She swallowed. "Tell me."

He cocked his head. "I'm not the best story-teller. Why don't I show you instead?"

CHAPTER 13

Once again, the world around Phoenyx changed. The sand on which she sat melted away and hardened into dark brown wood panels, radiating out to their limits where they met perpendicular stained papered walls that grew up a few meters. A wood paneled ceiling that, as it materialized closed, stole away the blue of the sky and the warmth of the sun.

They now sat in a cold, dank rectangular room that stank of mildew and body odor. All evidence of the beach they were at was gone; the happy voices snuffed out and replaced by the sound of thunder beyond the tiny windows. Lily and Skylar were nowhere in sight. All around them, the large empty room was filled with rickety bunk beds covered by dirty sheets and dirty clothes in piles on the floor and tattered stuffed animals with missing eye buttons lying about. Old calcified pipes snaked through places in the ceiling from the floor above and slither down along the walls and back into the floor.

"Where are we now?" she asked, looking all around.

"This is the foster home where Skylar and I grew up," he answered.

"This is a foster home? There are so many beds." She counted. "There were ten of you living here? Isn't there some kind of limit to how many children can stay in one home? Or at least in one room?"

"I'm sure there are, but our foster parents had ways of staying under the radar."

Just then, the sound of footsteps rumbled from up the stairs, and a herd of young boys emerged from them and into the room. Scampering to the bunk bed Phoenyx and Sebastian were sitting in front of were a pair of small boys. It was easy to see that they were young Sebastian and Skylar. Young Sebastian had the same raven black hair, all tousled about his head; the same blue eyes that shone like topaz stones with his innocence; and an unbelievably adorable face with pinch-able pink cheeks and an optimistic smile. He had to be the cutest little kid she had ever seen.

Young Skylar was a thousand times dorkier than adult Skylar. He wore large bug-eye glasses with thick brims that screamed Poindexter, and the super blond hair and pasty white skin didn't help at all. What a surprise that Skylar turned out looking so handsome!

Thunder cracked and lightening lit up the sky and flashed light through the tiny windows around the room. Several of the boys jumped, and Phoenyx tried to hide the fact that it made her jump too. But young Sebastian and Skylar were laughing and playing with action figures like they were the only ones in the room, their play unable to be disturbed.

Or so it seemed.

Stomps traveled down the stairs and a rotund, homely little girl trounced in with an equally unattractive woman and an unshaven, sloppy man in tow.

"He's the one who took it, Daddy," the little girl proclaimed, pointing an accusing finger at young Skylar.

Young Sebastian and Skylar put down their toys and put their full attention on all the fuss.

"The blond one?" the man asked. "Are you sure, punkin'?"

"Yes, Daddy, I saw him take it with my own two eyes," the girl said, crossing her arms and stomping one foot.

"Took what?" Sebastian demanded.

Skylar kept quiet. He looked dismayed, like if he said anything he would get himself into deeper trouble.

"Look at his face. See? The boy knows what you're talkin' about," the woman said angrily.

"So, you ungrateful little brat," the man trod aggressively toward young Skylar. "You think it's okay to steal from me, huh?"

"I didn't steal anything from you," young Skylar protested meekly.

"Don't lie to me, boy," the man yelled, pointing a stern finger at young Skylar. "Cynthia saw you take the fifty dollar bill out of my wallet, so I know it was you."

"I'm not lying; it wasn't me," young Skylar insisted. "She's the one who's lying. She took it."

The little girl sneered at him.

"How dare you accuse my little girl of stealing," the man said. "She has no reason to steal from me; I get her whatever she wants because she's a good little girl. But you, all of you, are good-for-nothing little brats."

"We're good enough to keep around so the state can fill your pockets," young Sebastian spat, his British accent sounding even sharper.

"What did you say?" The man looked very dangerous now. Phoenyx felt an innate need to protect the two children, even though she knew they were beyond her reach, that whatever danger was about to come to them already happened years ago.

Young Skylar stepped in front of young Sebastian. "But she did steal your money. She took it because she wanted to get the new Aaron Carter CD you told her she couldn't have."

The little girl's eyes were murderous now as they stared at young Skylar. The man turned around and looked at his daughter for any sign of truth in what young Skylar said.

"He's lying, Daddy," the girl shouted. "That's all they do: lie and steal. It's time to teach them a lesson and make them stop!"

"No, I swear; I'm not lying!" young Skylar urged.

"That's it; I'm tired o' this," the man said. He grabbed young Skylar's wrists hard and jerked him. "Where is it? Just give it to me and your punishment will be less bad."

"Leave him alone," young Sebastian yelled. He grabbed the man's arm but the man easily shook him off. He landed on his butt on the floor.

Again, Phoenyx felt compelled to jump in and help the boys but she knew it wasn't real. This was like watching a scary movie in 3-D—all she could do was watch the bad things happen.

"I don't have it, please," young Skylar pleaded.

"Fine!" The man raised his hand threateningly.

"Don't you touch him," young Sebastian yelled.

Phoenyx covered her eyes.

Suddenly, the pipes that snaked around this room burst at just about every joint all at once, spitting out water everywhere and instantly soaking everything. The sound scared everyone more than any of the previous thunder had, and now they all tried to shelter themselves from the raining pipes.

"Ahh, dammit to hell!" the man said, dropping young Skylar's wrist to shield his face. "Look at this place! I think it's raining more in here than it is out there."

"Daddy, I'm getting soaked!" the little girl complained.

"Come on, punkin'. Let's go upstairs," the woman said, leading the girl away from the showering pipe above their heads.

"I'm gonna go turn the damn water off," the man grumbled. "And you…" He pointed at young Skylar. "…as punishment, you are gonna clean up this mess." He stomped up the stairs, muttering to himself, "Don't know how the hell we can afford to fix these damn pipes now…damn kids stealing my money."

"Are you okay?" young Sebastian asked young Skylar just before the two boys faded away, along with the spurting water and all the other children who were watching.

The water that had soaked Phoenyx's clothes and hair disappeared, too, leaving her once again dry, even though she knew that the feeling of being wet was just an illusion, as well.

"You made the pipes burst," she said.

"I think maybe I did," adult Sebastian answered. "I always just thought that maybe God or someone up there was doing us a favor. You say that you felt it when you started that fire. I think I felt something when those pipes burst. I was overwhelmed with anger, at the way they were about to hurt my only friend, and still at the fact that my parents were gone. I felt so helpless. I wanted to be strong, to be powerful, so I wouldn't be stepped on anymore. That's all what I felt when those pipes burst."

"How old were you then?" she asked.

"Almost nine," he said.

"Oh, you poor thing," she said. "Poor Skylar too. Your foster parents were awful people. I wanted so much to beat the hell out of that man."

"Trust me, I had that dream many times when I lived there."

"That despicable little girl," she sneered.

"Cynthia always caused us problems," he said. "I think she had a crush on Skylar and wasn't used to not getting what she wanted. Being the only natural child in a house full of foster kids is even worse than being just an only child, apparently."

"What an awful place," she said. "Did they ever hit you?"

"No, that was the only time he ever came close to hitting one of us. If he ever hit Skylar or me, I don't know what I would have done but I wouldn't have let him forget it."

Overcome with affection and sympathy, she hugged him before she knew what she was doing. When she realized that her arms were touching the bare, wonderfully soft, yet firm skin of his back because his shirt was off, she removed herself, embarrassed.

"Sorry," she said awkwardly.

"No problem," he said, looking a little embarrassed himself but not dropping his hands from her waist.

Their eyes met for the first moment of silence that she enjoyed. All she wanted to do was put her arms around him again. But their moment was all too short.

A loud clank broke through the illusion and, too quickly, the illusion ripped away. They were back in their cells, the two of them pressed up against the bars that divided them. Skylar and Lily stood only a foot or so away from either of them, obviously interrupted from a conversation of their own.

The clank was followed by another and the door opened, demanding all their attention. *Has Lucas returned to set us free?* Phoenyx's heart leapt with hope for an instant.

She dropped back down when she saw a different man enter. He held a cloth bag of some kind, maybe a pillow case, filled with something large and round, stained at the bottom and dripping something dark. He threw it at the cells and closed the door again.

Skylar instantly backed away and put his hand over his mouth, face turning pale.

Sebastian crawled to the edge of the cell and stuck his hand through the bars to inspect the strange package. He pulled the cloth away, revealing the single most horrifying thing Phoenyx had ever seen with her own eyes—Lucas's severed head! The words "Nice Try" were written on his large forehead in black permanent marker.

Lily screamed at the top of her lungs and Skylar rushed to the toilet to puke.

Sebastian immediately moved to cover the head back up, then stuck his leg through the bars to kick it as far away from them as possible.

Lily's screaming continued and turned into weeping. Skylar stayed hunched over the toilet with his head resting on one arm while the other wrapped around his stomach. Sebastian and Phoenyx only kept looking at each other because they didn't want to look at anything else. She knew they were both thinking the same thing: they were screwed.

No one said anything in some time. No one could say anything. Lucas was their only hope to escape and, because of what she compelled him to do, this cult killed him—if only for the purpose of making a point to the four of them—that there was no way out. So that was yet another death on her hands. She was racking up quite a list, getting quite a few notches on her belt. At least she knew she didn't have to feel as guilty for this one. If she hadn't compelled him, he would have been perfectly content to see her and her friends die. Still, seeing that head meant these people were serious and twisted. She knew such acts of violence and brutality were possible, that they happened out in the world every day, but to actually see such an act committed was horrible—a truth she'd never forget.

In three days, they would die. Three days to suffer in this cell without food or water, three days to mourn the life about to be stolen from her and to mourn the people she was leaving behind. Her poor mom—first she lost her husband and now she would lose her daughter. She would be all alone in the world.

Sebastian slipped his hand through the bars and put it in hers. At least she would have three more days to spend with Sebastian. What a shame that she got to meet him now, like this, only to have him taken away. She knew she was falling for him; why bother denying it anymore? She felt a connection to him that first night they met, even before she remembered dreaming about him, before she knew anything about him. Knowing that fate brought them together, in this life and in who knows how many previous lives, was ruined by the thought that they would never meet in a future one ever again if the stupid ritual succeeded.

"You know what? No," she said, suddenly inspired. "We are not going to die here. There's got to be another way."

They all came out of their ruminations to look at her.

"How?" Lily asked, voice dry. "These people are monsters."

"Remember what Lucas said—that because of this solar storm our powers would get stronger?" Phoenyx said. "Let's use that to our advantage. Let's hone in on our abilities and strengthen them until we can use them as weapons. We have three days to practice."

The other three exchanged looks, the tiniest spark of hope twinkling in their eyes.

"Come to think of it, I have felt a buzz all day," Skylar said. "Like there's a static current running through my whole body."

"You know, it makes sense that you would feel the effects of the solar storm first," Phoenyx said. "You're Air, your element is closest to the sun."

He pursed his lips and nodded. "That does make sense."

"I'm sure the rest of us will feel it soon, too," Phoenyx said.

"Okay, so how do you propose we solve the initial problem of getting out of this cell?" Sebastian asked.

"I think our best bet to do that is for Skylar to attempt to bend the bars with his telekinesis," she said. "None of us is strong enough to do anything like that by hand, but air can be a powerful force. If you train, you might be able to do it. Like working out a muscle, it gets stronger the more you push it. It's time to start working out that brain, Skylar."

"All right, it's a worth a try," Skylar said.

"Then we just need to figure out how to get out of this room once we get out of these cells," Phoenyx pondered.

"Oh, that's simple," Skylar said. "I can unlock the door with my mind from the inside. It's a simple latch lock. I couldn't do that with the cell door because it's electronic."

Phoenyx raised her brows in understanding and nodded. "Great! Takes care of that."

"What about the rest of us?" Lily asked.

"Yeah," Sebastian said. "What are we going to do?"

"Once we get out of this room, we can put all of our abilities to use," Phoenyx said. "Skylar can use his telekinesis to push people away from us or hurt them any way necessary. I'll use my influence to compel people to help us or whatever opportunities I see along the way. Sebastian, you can use fear against them. Just like that story you told us, about your first time creating an illusion, make them see anything that will scare them off."

"Okay, I can do that," he said. "But that's a very passive way to go about it. I'll need a backup plan in case they don't scare easily."

"Then you can hone in on your water element," she said.

His eyes wandered as he took a moment to think about it. "Hmm, I just don't see how I can use water as a weapon...especially here, in a place like this. Sure, I can see how a whole dam filled with water would be a destructive force, but the only water we have access to is what's left in our water bottles."

"Actually, that's not the only water," she corrected. "Remember what you showed me earlier tonight? I'm sure there are pipes filled with running water all over this place. You just have to get creative. Since we will need the water bottles for drinking, you can practice with the one source of running water we have available." She looked at the toilet.

He sighed loudly. "Okay, I'll see what I can come up with."

"What about me?" Lily asked. "None of my abilities can be used as a weapon. I'm pretty much exactly the opposite of a weapon."

Phoenyx thought for a moment. "Maybe that's exactly what we need you to be. You're our protection. If one of us gets hurt, you're our guarantee it won't be permanent. You're our guarantee we'll all get out of here alive and in one piece."

That perked Lily right up.

"I think you are forgetting our biggest weapon of all," Sebastian said.

"What's that?" Phoenyx asked.

"You," he said.

"Me? No, I already said I could use my compulsion as a defense for us."

"I'm not talking about your compulsion," he said. "Phoenyx, you have the most destructive ability of all us. You can make fire. If you learn to master that ability—or at least control it—in the next three days, you're the best chance we have of escaping."

Everything he said brought back her fear. Her heart raced and the sweat broke out on her forehead.

She shook her head. "No, I can't do that. Mm-hm. No."

"He has a point," Skylar said. "So far, our best hope is that I can make my telekinesis strong enough to hurt people. That may take some time. If you think about it in terms of elements, how fast does air have to be going to cause any damage? Like sixty miles an hour at least, which is rare. But fire is a destructive element because it can damage even in its weakest state. You barely spark a match and you're destroying hundreds of molecules. We have to at least consider it."

She kept shaking her head. "What if I hurt someone again? What if I hurt one of you by accident?"

Sebastian put both his hands on her shoulders. "I know you won't." He smiled encouragingly. "If, by some chance, another accident happens—like you said, we have Lily for protection."

Lily nodded eagerly and Phoenyx let out a defeated laugh.

She had absolutely no faith in her so-called fire power. She had only just accepted its existence a few hours ago, and all she knew about it was that it was wild and out of control the one time she had ever used it. Could they risk letting it out again? If she hurt one of them, she would never forgive herself.

However, maybe they did have a point. Fire was definitely the most harmful thing in their arsenal. If they wanted a weapon out of the four elements, fire was the obvious choice. She had three days to learn to control it, and in here, three days was a long time. She couldn't ask them to practice using their powers if she wasn't willing to commit to the same thing.

"All right, I'll try to get a handle on the whole fire thing," she said. "Once I do, I will *only* use it as a last resort. I won't...I won't take another life if I don't have to."

"Okay," the three of them chorused.

"Since we don't know what time on the fourth day they plan to do the ritual, we should plan on making our escape attempt on the third day," Skylar said.

"You're right," Phoenyx said. "So that means we really only have tomorrow and the next day to prepare ourselves. We have to make every second count."

"I don't know about you guys but, after seeing..." Lily looked sideways at the bag in the corner, "...*that*, I won't be going to sleep any time soon."

"Yeah, me either," Skylar agreed, his face still tinted slightly green.

"I don't think I'll be able to sleep at all knowing I'm about to be killed," Sebastian said. "So let's start training now; although I'm not exactly sure how to start."

Lily looked at the pile of wadded up paper bags, picked one up and tossed it to Phoenyx.

"You can try to light the paper on fire," Lily said. "Paper is super flammable so that will be the best thing for you to practice with."

Phoenyx looked at the brown paper wad in her hands. Why did this make her feel like she was just given the most harrowing homework assignment of her life?

"Okay," she said as she exhaled. "Let's take our stations. I got the paper. Sebastian, you got the toilet—"

"Yay," he said unenthusiastically.

"Take your pick of the bars," Phoenyx said to Skylar. She turned back to the wad in her hands. "Let's get started."

Phoenyx crossed her legs and tried to get comfortable. But, really, how comfortable can one get just after learning someone was killed because of them and in three days or so they will be next? *Okay, focus. All you have to do is...start this piece of paper on fire with your mind. How hard can it be?*

She stared at the paper and tried to put everything else out of her mind. Maybe she just had to visualize it. Like Sebastian's ability, maybe she just had to picture the paper starting on fire. She imagined it once, then again more vividly. Nothing happened.

Hmm. Okay, maybe it was something more like Peter Pan, think happy thoughts. Happiness was a positive and powerful thing, right? She thought about how much she would love to have a full course meal right now. Oh, even better, how great a buffet would be. She could eat and eat and eat and make the hunger pains wish they never existed. Nope, that only made her stomach growl loudly.

That's not going to work. All right, don't think about superficial happiness, think about what would make you truly happy. To see Mom again. She thought of coming home to her mom, giving her a huge, very long hug and telling her all the things she never said, like what a great mom she was and how she did a great job raising her on her own for the past six years.

That made her think of her dad. Now to see him alive would make her extremely happy. She imagined him coming back into her life with open arms, telling her the one thing she would love to hear: that he forgave her.

Crap; that just brought the aching fear and guilt back.

She sighed, then looked around the room to see how the others were doing.

Lily sat in the corner staring at her last apple, probably quarreling with herself over whether to sate her hunger now or save it for when she really needed it. Skylar stared, no, scowled at the bars in front of him, looking like his eyes were about to pop out of his head. Sebastian was perched in a hover over the toilet, staring apathetically into the water.

He was so cute. He had his white button-down shirt just hanging on his shoulders, the buttons all unbuttoned so his shirt was open to reveal just a bit of his bare chest. He definitely had a swimmer's chest. He looked like one of those surfer gods one sees running down a beach in slow motion on a TV show.

A new, warm feeling replaced the guilt and fear in her stomach, and she remembered something that should have been obvious right from the start. Her compulsion ability, it stemmed from sensuality. Whenever she made someone do something, she would feel the sensation of being turned on. If lust was what fueled that power, it only made sense that it would fuel her fire power, too!

"Duh," she whispered.

"What?" Sebastian asked.

"Oh, uh, nothing," she said.

While their gazes were on each other, he smiled at her.

Maybe it was time she stopped pushing away the thoughts that lay in wait all this time. She had so many reasons for fighting them off before—they just met, their lives were in danger, there were more important things to worry about, there were bars between them so there was no point in torturing herself with something she couldn't have, etc. However, this might be her key to unlocking the Fire within her.

When he went back to concentrating on the water, she concentrated on him. God, he had such perfect lips—so pink and full and seemingly soft. She wanted to kiss them since the night they first talked. He was probably a great kisser. He was probably great at a lot of things. She let her eyes wander down his neck and to his open shirt. Now that she wasn't fighting it, she could really enjoy his chest—just the right amount of muscles, not too buff and not too scrawny. He shifted his position where he sat and his shirt moved just enough to reveal one very perky, hard nipple. For the first time, she appreciated that it was cold in here. Yet, she was getting very warm.

Oh, to hell with it! She let herself fall into a fevered fantasy of what would happen if these bars didn't separate them and Lily and Skylar weren't here. She imagined crawling over to him and surprising him with a teasing kiss, only enough to let him know what she wanted, so that he would pull her against him and open his mouth to let his tongue do the talking. Oh, how amazing it would feel to kiss him passionately and hungrily!

She would pull his shirt all the way off and let her hands roam eagerly all over his naked back. He would pull hers up over her head, then snap her bra off with one flick of his fingers and toss it to the side. Then he would pull her up and cover one of her breasts with his hungry mouth while his hand playfully covered the other. She would run her fingers through his thick black hair, holding him against her. They would wrestle each other down to the floor and let their hands find what they really wanted—the buttons to each other's pants. Oh, she blushed at the thought of what waited under that black polyester for her.

Suddenly, Skylar cleared his throat awkwardly and loudly. *Oh, right, Skylar's a mind reader. Oops. How awkward for him.*

Phoenyx stopped her fantasy but her entire body was warm and hungry, and not for food, which was a welcome change. She looked back down at the paper she held. Letting her lust flow through her hand, sounds from her fantasy echoing in her mind, she said clearly in her mind, "Burn."

As she watched, thin smoke wafted and swirled upward.

Holy shit, it worked!

The smoke stopped, its death almost tangible, like she felt it with some unknown sense she couldn't locate.

"Holy hell, Phoenyx, is that smoke?" Sebastian asked excitedly. "You're actually doing it!"

"Oh, uh...yeah, I did," she said, trying to compose her voice. "I had it but it wasn't strong enough."

Damn, looking at him now made her ache. Sure, that's just what she needed, more aches. Maybe giving into her lust and letting herself want him was a bad idea. Not to mention the discomfort of knowing that Skylar saw everything she was thinking about his best friend.

"At least you're getting started," Sebastian said. "I am getting nowhere with this water thing. I thought maybe it would be like my illusions, that if I imagined the water moving or something, it would move. All I see happening is an illusion of the water moving, not the water actually moving."

"Huh, that's frustrating," she said. She swallowed and tried to get moisture back in her mouth.

"Anyone have any suggestions?" he asked.

"Nope," Skylar said. "I'm getting nowhere too. I think that trying to bend the bars right away is the wrong way to go about this. I think I need to start with moving or lifting something lighter, then move my way up. Like Phoenyx said, it's like working out—you start with the smaller weights first. Right?"

"You can try with me," Lily said, setting aside the apple she'd been staring at for the past hour. "I don't have anything to do and, if I don't find something to preoccupy myself with soon, I'm going to eat that stupid apple and really regret it after I really enjoy it. So use me as your weight. See if you can lift me."

"All right; sure. Why not?" Skylar welcomed.

He moved to right in front of the bars and sat in the same position as before, which was apparently his focused position, with his legs crossed, his back hunched forward a bit, and his elbow resting on his knee with his hand holding his chin.

* * * *

After about two hours of focusing, Skylar managed to levitate Lily about an inch off the ground. The effort of it pretty much knocked him after that. Lily was already falling asleep before that so she was happy to lay down when Skylar called it quits.

Sebastian was still wide awake, looking into the water not like he was concentrating on it but more like he was daydreaming. Unfortunately, Phoenyx was unable to think of anything but him since she let the desire in. She tried sparking the paper a few times but all she got was smoke that didn't last long.

"So visualizing the water moving doesn't work, huh?" she asked, moving closer.

"Not even a little bit," he said. "I assumed that would be the key because it works for the illusions."

"Hmm," she hummed, thinking. "I have an idea. When those pipes burst at your foster home, you said you felt it. What exactly did you feel?"

"I wanted to protect Skylar but I was so small and helpless. I wanted to stop Gus from hurting him. I wanted to hurt Gus."

"If I remember right from what you showed me, the pipes all burst in your direction, didn't they?" she mused. "I mean, usually when pipes rupture naturally, the fracture is all around the pipe, or at least at random places on the pipe, wherever the weak spots are. Don't you think it means something that they all burst aimed at you and Gus?"

He thought about it. "Okay. So, what are you saying?"

"I think the way to control the water is by seeing it as an extension of yourself," she said. "You wanted to do something to stop Gus and then the water around you rushed out toward you, toward Gus. The water acted as your extra limbs. Maybe you should try moving the water as if it were a physical part of you."

"Hmm. That's how Skylar says his telekinesis works," he said. "All right, let's see if it works."

He looked into the water. A few minutes passed. Phoenyx lifted herself with her knees to see into the bowl. Suddenly, the center of the water's surface bubbled up and stretched like a misshapen arm reaching up.

"Oh, my God, I did it!" Sebastian gasped. Then the water deflated and smoothed itself back to a flat surface.

"That was great!" Phoenyx praised. "You're one step closer to mastering it!"

"You were totally right; I had to actively move the water like it was a hand that had fallen asleep," he said. "I just had to make the neural connection. I never would have figured it out without you. I would have stared into this damn toilet like an idiot for the next two days." He laughed.

Phoenyx smiled. Then she looked again at the other two slumbering cell mates. They were both asleep now, so nothing she could think, or do, would offend either of them. She should take advantage of this opportunity.

"I'm glad I could help," Phoenyx said. "Now, maybe you could help me out."

"Sure, what can I do?" he asked.

"Well, do you remember how it felt when I touched you and compelled you to kiss Skylar?" she asked.

He smiled knowingly and raised an eyebrow in a very sexy expression. "How could I forget?"

She giggled, heart fluttering at what she was about to propose. "I thought, like you did with your illusions, that the thing fueling my first power might be what fuels my element too. I tried it but all I can get is smoke."

He nodded, a sultry mist glossing over his gorgeous blue eyes. "Interesting."

"I'd like to try something," she braved. "If you'd let me." She reached her hand through the bars, beckoning him.

He scooted closer, taking her hand. She pulled him in as she pressed herself against the bars. With just enough space between two cold bars, their lips met. Oh, his lips were even softer than they looked! Her lust flooded through her and she didn't bother to stop it from flowing through their connecting parts to pass into him.

He moaned with the rush of it. His mouth opened and his tongue came out to play. Their arms wrapped around each other, grasping and tugging, squashing them against the bars that only barely divided them. They kissed ravenously, lips wrestling, tongues dancing in an endless struggle to satisfy an itch that just could not be scratched.

When her lust was at a peak that was too much to bear, she broke from his oh-so-delicious mouth and picked up the paper bag. "*Burn*," she commanded. The bag burst into flames and Sebastian flinched away from the heat of it. Like her lust, the flames were insatiable and devoured the bag in seconds, leaving nothing but ashes in her open palm.

"Wow." Sebastian panted heavily.

"It worked." She breathed triumphantly. She rested her forehead against Sebastian's, both of them gripping the bars to keep themselves up, both trying to catch their breath.

One of his hands found hers and they entwined their fingers around the bar. He rubbed his nose against hers, his lips so close but not touching. The desire was so strong and yet equally repellant, for they both knew that if they started kissing again, they wouldn't be able to stop. The kissing wouldn't be enough to placate them but it would be all they could do. Making out would be such sweet torment.

"That was...incredible," Sebastian said through breaths. He swallowed. "Thank you *so much* for letting me be your guinea pig."

She laughed. "I'm just glad that Lily and Skylar went to sleep. I have been thinking about you nonstop for hours. I just had to try the real thing."

He groaned longingly and bit his lip. Then he cupped one side of her face with his hand. "I wish these bars weren't between us."

She nuzzled her face into his hand, wanting more of his touch. "I know; me too." She kissed the base of his thumb.

He leaned back and it looked like it took every ounce of his strength to do so, jaw clenched and exhaling deeply.

"As much as I would *love* to keep practicing with you like this," he said, "I don't think lust is the answer to unlocking your element. When we go out there, when we have to start fighting, I think that sex will be the last thing on your mind, and you won't be able to kiss me every time you need to defend yourself."

"Oh." She sighed, disappointed.

"The fire that you started in your house happened because you were angry," he said. "I think anger will be a much more easily accessible emotion in a fight. I think that is the emotion we should be focusing on."

Anger. Why hadn't I realized that? Dammit. She really, really wanted a reason to kiss him more. But he was right. Come to think of it, when she started that fire years ago, she wasn't even touching the place that started on fire. So, it didn't necessarily have to be like her compulsion ability. She didn't have to touch what she wanted to burn for it to burn. That would definitely make it more useful if she had to defend herself.

"You're right," she said. "I'll practice with that tomorrow."

He nodded and took her chin between his thumb and index finger. "Besides, when we're kissing, I want it to be just because you want to kiss me."

She smiled, happy for his invitation to continue. "Oh, trust me, I want to."

She pulled him close and the frenzy started all over again.

The first thing Phoenyx saw when she opened her eyes was Sebastian's gorgeous face a few inches from hers. They were laying as close to each other as they comfortably could with the bars between them. He was still sleeping. *Damn, he is so cute, and last night was fantastic!* She felt all warm and cozy inside. She slept surprisingly well for a woman with a death sentence.

She sat up and yawned, stretching her arms up.

"Good morning," Lily said behind her, surprising her. "Or should I say good afternoon?"

Phoenyx looked around to see that Lily and Skylar were both awake. He was already in training mode; he was once again staring at Lily intently.

"Afternoon?" Phoenyx asked. "What time is it?"

Lily looked at her watch. "Almost one o'clock."

"Whoa, I can't believe I slept so long," Phoenyx said happily.

"I can't believe any of us slept at all," Lily said. She extended her hand holding an apple. There was a single bite taken out of it. "Here, you should have a bite. Just one so we can conserve."

"Thanks, Lil," Phoenyx said, feeling touched by Lily's consideration. She took the apple and took one big bite. Geez, she couldn't remember a time when an apple ever tasted this good. She took her time chewing, savoring, and moving it from side to side until the mush dissolved away. Then she gave the apple back to Lily, doubting her self-control.

As soon as she took the apple, Lily was suddenly lifted up a few inches off the floor and then fell hard back on her butt. Skylar let out a big breath and put his hand over his forehead soothingly.

"Ow!" Lily yipped.

"Sorry," Skylar said. "It's still hard to control. I'll try to be gentler."

"It's okay," Lily said. "It's my fault for having such a boney butt." She laughed, leaning to the side to rub one cheek.

Skylar chuckled and shook his head. "All right, I need a break." He took out an apple from his own reserve and bit into it.

Sebastian stirred. When he opened his eyes, he looked lost for a moment; then his eyes found Phoenyx and he smiled. He sat up and yawned, running his hands through his hair, seeming very rested and satisfied.

"Good morning," he said, giving Phoenyx an intimate look.

"Morning," she said back, giving him a Mona Lisa smile.

"Technically, its afternoon," Lily said.

"Oh, right," Phoenyx said, remembering that she and Sebastian were not alone. Then she remembered that, if it was one o'clock, she had wasted a whole morning's worth of training. *Crap! I need to get started now.*

"Sebastian, we need to get to training," she said. "We slept all morning, so we have a lot of catching up to do."

He breathed in deep through his nose. "Okay," he said. He looked at Skylar, snatched the apple from his hand, took a bite, and then handed it back before Skylar could gripe at him about it. With his mouth full, Sebastian smiled wide at him, then moved to his post in front of the toilet as he chewed the apple bite loudly.

Phoenyx followed her own instructions and took one of the paper bags from the pile. She sat back against the wall and crumpled up the bag into a ball in her hands, then set in on the floor in front of her; she knew she could start a fire by touching whatever she wanted to burn but she needed to learn to burn things without touching them. Okay, time to test Sebastian's anger theory. She had to get mad. What would make her mad?

Her eyes wandered over to Sebastian. He was looking at her too. She blushed and made that weird frown that comes from trying to hide a smile and looked away. How on earth was she going to get angry right now? She had just had one of the best nights ever. The only way it could have been better is if they could have fully explored their lust for each other. Her whole body blushed at the thought. Her mind was filled with thoughts of Sebastian, and it wasn't easily going to let go of them.

She looked at him again, and again he was looking at her. She smiled at him, and he winked at her, making her blush again.

"What's the winking all about?" Lily asked somewhat playfully. "What's going on over there?"

Sebastian and Phoenyx reluctantly broke eye contact to address Lily.

"They made out last night," Skylar said flatly.

"What?" Lily burst with a big open-mouthed smile.

Now both Phoenyx and Sebastian were blushing madly and fidgeting embarrassedly.

"Just so you both know, I'm trying as hard as I can to stay out of your minds. I'm still disgusted," Skylar said.

Phoenyx and Sebastian burst out laughing. Sebastian patted Skylar on the shoulder.

"Sorry, buddy, we'll try to keep things PG," he said.

Lily looked all bubbly and excited. "How did it happen?"

"I-I'll give you details later," Phoenyx assured in a hushed tone.

Lily smiled enthusiastically. Phoenyx could tell her new friend was mentally appraising Sebastian.

"All right, seriously," Skylar said, "can we all just please focus on the task at hand. It's hard enough to do this with silence, let alone trying to block out live streaming porn from both of your minds."

Another wink from Sebastian.

"You're right, Skylar," Phoenyx said. "You're right, we—" she looked at Sebastian—"need to cool things down. We need to focus."

"Yeah, we'll just wait till you fall asleep again," Sebastian teased Skylar.

Skylar laughed somewhat sardonically and shook his head, then closed his eyes and sat up straight in a meditative sort of position.

Phoenyx took a page from his book and did the same. She took a deep breath in and then whooshed it out. She grudgingly pushed Sebastian out of her mind and told her body to chill. This really was serious, and she didn't have time to daydream about Sebastian. Though she didn't want to, she had to learn how to control her element. She may end up needing it.

What was going to get her mad? She searched through her memories. The most recent one was the memory of prom night. She was furious at her ex-boyfriend that night. She expected some big romantic gesture and dolled herself up. Scott turned the night into a complete disaster. Not to mention he ruined her three-hundred dollar dress. Yep, she was still mad about it. This was good. She replayed every detail of that night, letting the anger it caused simmer. Stupid Scott and his stupid friends and stupid habits. It made her want to just punch his stupid face.

She opened her eyes, which were narrowed in a scowl, and stared at the paper.

Burn.

A smoke wisp floated out from the folds.

"Burn," she yelled in her head.

A longer smoke tail escaped.

That memory must not be good enough. She had to get angrier. She closed her eyes again and dug deeper. She focused on other memories: the time she tripped down the stairs and fractured her ankle and when they went to the hospital there was a huge wait and she had to deal with the pain for an hour and a half; the time she waited in line for Lady Gaga concert tickets for almost a full weekend and got to the teller just in time for them to be sold out, and then she had to hear everyone at school brag about how awesome the concert was; the time her friend Tracy crashed

Phoenyx's first car and made her promise to tell both their parents that it was Phoenyx's fault, then she got a boyfriend and stopped hanging out with Phoenyx anyway.

Nothing she could think of would create more than a short-lived ember and a few puffs of smoke. Memories weren't going to do it. They were too far in the past, they wouldn't deliver the kind of anger she needed. She needed something to make her mad right now in the present.

She looked around. She had a reason to be furious right in front of her, she was sitting in it. She was drugged and taken against her will, thrown into a tiny, cold room with three perfect strangers from whom she had absolutely no privacy, caged like an animal and starved for days— all only so that she could be ritually sacrificed like a Mayan virgin. Her three bedfellows, whom she had grown to love, would be killed alongside her. Lily, sweet and innocent Lily, who had such great potential and a family that would mourn her. Skylar, who even though he could be a bit of an intellectual snob sometimes, truly knew her and didn't run away from what he saw and, in fact, even liked it. Sebastian—sexy, charming, perfect Sebastian—who came into her life a little too late.

None of them deserved this. The people who were doing this were horrible, wicked sadists and deserved to be punished.

She opened her eyes and glared at the paper, feeling only her hatred for her captors. There was a spark and the outside of the paper caught fire. The bag crackled and filled the air with the smell of stale oil and burning paper. Her hatred grew, consuming her. Her breath quickened and the paper burned more rapidly. The fire shown with a luminescence that rivaled the overhead lights. She was faintly aware of a gasp from Lily, who wasn't too busy concentrating to see the fire.

Fragments of the night her dad died flashed in her mind—the rage she had felt, how dangerous she was then. Suddenly she realized it wasn't the fire that was dangerous, it was how swiftly her emotions raged and took hold of her. The hatred terrified her. She suddenly panicked and, just like her anger, the fire dwindled and snuffed out.

She lifted her foot and stepped on the partially burnt paper, sliding her foot against the ground until the paper was in shreds and ashes. Then she brushed the remnants to the side.

Even though the fire was out and her anger was gone, the panic didn't go away. All she saw were replayed images of her house burning, her dad's face. She had to shake this feeling before it consumed her again.

She decided to invest her attention in her friends and see if she could help them succeed where she was failing.

"Skylar, you're doing it!" Lily clapped. "This is amazing!" She hovered a foot off the floor, gleeful as Wendy on her way to Neverland. She leaned back, stretched out, and moved her limbs about—basking in the liberation of being no longer earthbound.

"That looks like so much fun," Phoenyx said. "I want to be next!"

"Oh sure, I've known you all this time and, now that we're about to die, you learn to make people fly," Sebastian complained to Skylar. "I think I should be next."

Skylar laughed. "You'll all get your turn. I just can't believe I can lift a whole person. I never imagined I could be this strong. Who knows what else I'll be able to do with a little practice?"

Lily slowly de-elevated back to sit on the floor. "That was a much better landing," she said. "I barely felt it."

"Okay, seriously, I want to be next," Phoenyx offered. "I need a break anyway."

"This is good; I can see if I can lift you both at the same time," Skylar said.

"Happy to help," Phoenyx said.

As she sat and talked with Lily while Skylar concentrated on using them as dumbwaiters, her panic receded. This day was full of emotions and she was spent. First, a morning full of longing; then, an afternoon full of anger and hatred—she was headed toward a night full of fear and regret. Talking with Lily about what TV shows they were missing right now was a welcome distraction. She was grateful that, for whatever reason, Lily didn't bring up that she saw Phoenyx successfully light the bag. Phoenyx told herself that she would try again tomorrow but the truth was she didn't want to. Every time she thought about using her power, her insides felt cold and sick, although that could just be the hunger. Even though she wouldn't admit it to herself, she knew deep down that, no matter what, she wasn't going to use her fire power. Not when they make their escape, not ever.

It was early morning on what would hopefully be their last day as prisoners. None of them slept through the night. Sometime around midnight, Skylar successfully levitated both Lily and Phoenyx a few feet off the ground. The feeling was amazing. It really was like flying. There was this feeling in Phoenyx's stomach, almost like the way it feels to be on a rollercoaster, that free-falling, up and down, tingly feeling. It was a good thing she didn't get motion sickness but, then again, her stomach was empty anyway so it wouldn't have mattered. It was very exciting to see Skylar's ability grow. She was certain he'd be able to bend the bars by the next day.

Sebastian's ability had grown much as well. He could make the water float straight out of the toilet bowl and move all around the room. Too bad he couldn't magically clean the water, too, because they were almost out of drinking water and she was getting desperately thirsty. If they had to stay in this room any longer, she would go for the water in the tank of the toilet.

Now they were all just relaxing and talking, taking a break in the place of sleep to regain some strength before starting again.

"I can definitely feel it now," Lily said. "It's a vibrating, fuzzy feeling all over. All the hairs on my arms are standing up, like I have goose bumps but I don't."

"Yeah, I feel it too," Sebastian said. "That solar storm is definitely building. Can you feel it?" he asked Phoenyx.

She took a moment to assess herself. Now that she thought about it, she did feel different. She thought it was just nerves, this electric buzz all through her. It felt similar to that initial feeling you get after a beer, before you are drunk. Only it didn't cloud her mind, at all, and it wasn't really a high feeling but not necessarily unpleasant either.

"Yes, I feel it," she said.

"I definitely feel more powerful," Sebastian said. "I can...I *feel* the water in all the pipes under the floor and in the walls. It's trippy as hell but really cool; I found a new sense I never knew I had."

"Be careful with it, though," Phoenyx cautioned jokingly. "You cause a leak in here and we might all drown."

"We all stink pretty badly and could all use a bath," he jibed.

"You aren't kidding," Skylar said. "You always act like a horse's ass and now you smell like one." He grinned teasingly.

Lily and Phoenyx laughed, secretly smelling themselves, and neither one happy with the results.

"I'm surprised you can smell anything with your nose so high up in the air like that," Sebastian retorted.

"You want to see up in the air, do you?" Skylar asked.

Suddenly, they were all picked up off the floor and hovering just under the ceiling.

"Whoa!" Phoenyx and Lily gasped in surprise.

"Bloody hell," Sebastian exclaimed, sounding extremely British just then. "That's goddamned amazing! You're lifting all of us at once!"

It wasn't just the four of them. All of the empty water bottles, paper bags, burger wrappers, and apple cores were floating all around them. Only hours ago, Skylar was barely able to lift two people and now he levitated everything in this room without breaking a sweat.

"That storm is definitely getting bigger," Skylar said. "I feel like I can do anything. I will definitely be able to bend those bars tomorrow morning. I'll bet all your powers are stronger too."

He set them all down softly.

"Why don't you try?" Sebastian asked Phoenyx. "If Skylar can do that, I can't wait to see what you can do."

His face was boyish and hopeful. Lily was smiling at her.

Phoenyx swallowed. She couldn't let them down. "Uh, sure. Let's see."

She took another paper bag and set it in front of her. She definitely felt a difference. She felt powerful. Just looking at the paper bag, she knew she could light it with no problem. It wanted to burn. It was begging to burn. It began to smoke. She felt their eyes on her and she wanted to just get it over with quickly, but it wouldn't do anything more than smoke. She pushed her will harder but nothing happened. Something was holding her back. Something was stopping this from working.

"I can't do it," she said. "For some reason, it's not working."

"Keep trying," Sebastian encouraged. "There was smoke just now. I saw you burn that paper yesterday. I know you can do this. Try again."

She tried. All she felt was cold and her heart skipped nervously. There wasn't even smoke this time. That humming inside her was strong and almost audible but something blocked it. Her heart beat even faster. It was like every time she would think, "*fire*," another part of her would blow it out.

"It's because you're scared," Skylar said. "Your fear is like a fire extinguisher, it slakes your power. That's how your arm got burnt." He nodded his head toward her right arm. "As soon as you became afraid of it, your power over the fire died and it started to burn you."

She clutched her wrist.

"What are you afraid of?" Lily asked. "Aside from the possibility of getting killed in two days but we're all afraid of that."

"Are you afraid of hurting one of us?" Sebastian asked. "If you do, Lily can heal us. None of us would blame you because we are all just getting used to our powers—none of us really knows what we're doing."

"It's not that," Phoenyx said. "I mean it's not just that. I'm afraid of losing control. The whole reason I started that damn fire was because I lost control of my emotions. When I use that power, whatever emotion I feel at the time just goes haywire. The fire feeds my emotions just as it feeds off what it's burning. What if one of these times I can't stop it and the fire just feeds and feeds until I don't recognize myself anymore?"

"I can't say that won't happen," Sebastian said. "But you're stronger than you give yourself credit for. You have a power that is stronger than the fire, stronger than your fear or any other emotion. That is your willpower. Not once since we've been down here have I seen you give up, even for a second."

"He's right," Lily said. "Right from the beginning, since we first woke up here, you've faced every terrible new thing head on. You've been my strength."

"I believe you can learn to control this," Sebastian continued. "Now you just have to believe it."

Phoenyx shrugged. "I'll try."

"I hope you do," Skylar said. "My telekinesis may be formidable but if we don't have your fire tomorrow, we will be wasting a valuable resource."

"No pressure or anything, but our lives depend on you," Sebastian taunted.

"Gee, thanks," Phoenyx frowned. "That makes me feel so much better."

"Good." He laughed. "Okay, I think we've had a long enough break. Let's get to it." He put his hand on Phoenyx's shoulder. "I'm here if you need any help."

"I know." She smiled.

He squeezed her shoulder, then went back to his post. She went back to hers. Nothing they said really helped. She still didn't want to use her power. Hopefully, she wouldn't have to. Still, she would practice with it for now, for their benefit. They all deserved as much.

* * * *

Caloric

The day came to an end. The last day they would spend in this room, for better or worse. They all had a bite or two of their last apple, with just enough left for one more bite for each of them in the morning. There was no more water and, after having only small bits of very dry apple, Phoenyx was absolutely parched. She had no idea of the true meaning of the word 'parched' until this moment. She was looking at cotton-mouth in the rearview mirror.

Lily was curled up in the corner and Skylar lay on his back near the opposite wall, both of them trying to get to sleep. Once again, Sebastian and Phoenyx were sitting against the wall next to each other on either side of the bars, the late night talkers. Not that anyone could tell the difference between night and day in here but her circadian rhythm had adjusted to give her an inkling of time, finally.

She was so nervous about tomorrow. Talking about escaping was easy. Anything *still to come* is easy but they were right on the precipice. Seven or so hours from now, they would break out of this room and brave whatever obstacles await them on the other side of that door. Though the knowledge that no one out there could kill them just yet was a slight comfort, that didn't mean they were safe from incapacitating injury as well. She had to stop being so morbid if she was ever going to get tired enough to sleep, and she had to sleep tonight to have strength enough for tomorrow.

"What are you thinking about?" Sebastian asked. "You've been quiet for too long."

"The same thing we're all thinking about." She sighed. "Distract me."

"All right." He laughed. "Rather than thinking about what could go wrong tomorrow, think about how great it will be to finally get out of here. The four of us will all go out and celebrate. You and I can finally go on that date."

She smiled. "That's right. Just what did you have in mind for our first date?"

"A nice restaurant, a bottle of wine, then maybe some mini-golf—"

"Ha ha, wow, I haven't played mini-golf since my ex-boyfriend took me on our first date," she said. "So, I'm guessing that's a classic first date activity for guys, huh?"

"Of course," Sebastian said. "Well, really any game where we can come up behind a girl and put our arms around her with the pretense of teaching her how to play: mini-golf, bowling, pool—you name it."

"Ha, ha, ha!" She laughed a little too loudly and remembered that Lily and Skylar were trying to sleep. She put her finger up to her lips and shushed.

"So, what happened between you and your old boyfriend?" Sebastian whispered.

She scoffed. "He turned my prom night into a nightmare."

"Yes, you've said that," he said. "I know there's a story there and it's not like we don't have time for it."

She shrugged. "All right, I'll tell you. First thing you have to understand is that, even though it's juvenile and silly, prom meant a lot to me. For the first time in pretty much my entire school career, I had more than one friend, and prom was basically my last chance to be a part of that group before we all graduated and went off to different colleges. My mom and I went in together on a really nice expensive dress from the same catalogue as my girlfriends who were going. Normally I don't care that much about clothes but, as I've said, this was a big deal to me; my dress cost three hundred dollars.

"So anyway, I got all dressed up and was expecting Scott to make the night romantic for me if he had any hope of us trying the whole long distance thing. We planned for him to show up in a limo. When he knocked on my door, all that was outside was his crappy jeep with the word 'prom!' written all over the windows in florescent marker. Our two friends John and Amy were in the backseat.

"'You look beautiful,' he said.

"'Thanks. Uh, what happened to the limo?' I asked.

"'Oh, I called in too late and they were out of limos,' he said. 'But I promise, the jeep will be just as good.' Then he held up a long stem red rose and I thought, '*well at least he got the tuxedo and the rose right.*'

"So, we got in the car and started driving; and then he got a phone call. I didn't really pay attention to anything he said. I just assumed he was talking to our other friends who were already there. But then we made a turn onto the highway, which was going in the opposite direction of school.

"'Where are we going?' I asked.

"'We're just making a quick stop,' he said. 'We're getting some, uh, party supplies.' He winked at John in the rearview mirror. John then slapped the back of Scott's seat and started howling like a moron. I knew they both had a thing for pot and even did some of the harder stuff like coke sometimes. Most of the time it didn't bother me, but it did irk me a bit that we were putting off prom to get whatever drug they wanted.

"So we drove fifteen minutes out of town to some house in the woods. There was a huge party going on there and cars parked everywhere. Scott and John said they would be right back so Amy and I waited in the car. After about five minutes, we decided to go inside and look for them so we could leave. Everyone at the party stared at us like we were freaks the whole time we were inside. Some of the especially drunk girls were falling over themselves to touch our dresses and tell us how pretty we looked in them. When we finally found the guys, they were in the back yard, sniffing lines off a piece of cardboard with some older thug looking guys.

"'It's time to go,' I told Scott.

"'Yeah, come on,' Amy said, tugging on John's arm.

"'Just one more minute, babe' Scott said.

"It was right then that red and blue lights flashed all around and sirens sounded. Everyone went crazy and started scattering. Scott and John grabbed our hands and pulled us through the side gate of the backyard to get to the jeep. Cars were taking off left and right and we jumped in the jeep and started to drive away, and cop cars started following everyone off the property. We were all freaking out and yelling at Scott. He did the smart thing and turned really sharp down a side road that went into the woods. Just when we thought we were safe, the car sputtered and died.

"I really started yelling at Scott then, telling him how he really should have gotten a limo and how I couldn't believe he dragged us all the way out there. We heard sirens in the distance so we couldn't just wait there. We pushed the jeep off to the side and ran through the woods in the direction we thought the main road was. By the time we got back to town, my dress was covered in mud and the bottom was ripped up all in shreds, and prom was over. So I broke up with him that night and felt about a hundred and seventy pounds lighter ever since.

"So much for wanting romance, huh?"

"Wow, that's pretty messed up," Sebastian said. "I'm sorry you didn't get the prom you wanted... What did your prom dress look like? Just so I have an idea of what a three-hundred dollar dress looks like. Paint a picture for me."

"Uh, let's see, it was lavender chiffon with gold lace at the top, sleeveless with a sweetheart neck line, and it had a long flowing skirt that went all the way down to the floor," she summarized.

He nodded. "Okay. So, something like this?"

Out of the corner of her eye, she noticed a color change on her lap. She looked down and saw the blue jeans she had been wearing for a week turned into a shimmering two-toned lavender chiffon skirt. Her rather odorous tear-stained black cotton T-shirt became a tight fitting lavender bodice that shaped her breasts perfectly and left her shoulders bare.

"Oh, my God!" she exclaimed.

When she looked back up, she was no longer in her prison, but in a large gymnasium decorated with hanging pastel streamers all over the ceiling. No more of the painfully bright florescent lights; the whole gym was dimmed, lit only by different colored accent lights. She looked at Sebastian and saw that he was now adorned in a wonderfully fitted tuxedo.

"Wha—" was all she could muster.

Sebastian stood up and offered her his hand. "I figured since you never got to your prom, and this might be our last night alive, I'll bring the prom to you. Can I have this dance?" The song "*At Last*" began to play.

Phoenyx felt her face light up. She took his hand and let him pull her up. Still holding her hand, he put his other hand around her waist. She put her arms around the back of his neck and they began to dance.

"You are just full of surprises," she said. "The song couldn't be more perfect. Do you know that this song is at the end of just about all of my favorite romance movies?"

He smiled so handsomely. "How did I do with everything else? I've never been to a high school prom so I just had to wing it."

"It's perfect," she said. "I wouldn't change a thing."

"Hmm, we may have a problem," he said, biting his lip. She cocked her head curiously, and he said, "I think I made your dress too sexy because you are killing me in it." She threw her head back and laughed, then drew him near and kissed him.

When they managed to stop kissing, she said, "Thank you for this. I couldn't imagine a better way to spend what could be the last night of my life."

"Thank you," he said, "for turning out to be so amazing. If things do turn out for the worst tomorrow, I wouldn't regret any of this because I got to meet you." They held each other's eyes for a moment, then she put her head on his shoulder and just swayed with him. She wanted to savor every second of this, to enjoy it to the fullest. She never wanted to let him go. Whatever happens tomorrow, at least they had tonight.

"Since this might be our last night together," he started after a while, "there's something I want you to know." He pulled away just enough to look at her, still keeping the dance going. "I...I dreamt about you before we met."

Her heart warmed.

"I know," she said. "That night when you and Skylar were talking about it, I was still awake and heard by accident."

He blushed and closed his eyes in embarrassment. "Oh God; all this time, you knew and didn't say anything?" He laughed, getting more embarrassed by the minute. "I can't believe you heard all that. You must have thought I was crazy."

She also laughed. "It's okay. Actually, I didn't think you were crazy because I've dreamt about you too."

The embarrassment left his face. They shared a look of complete understanding and acceptance.

"We both dreamt about each other before we met," he said. He lifted one hand to caress her cheek, and she melted into his touch. "So, it is as I thought, as I hoped...we have met in other lives before this one."

She nodded. "Or at least one. I think the one I dream about was our life before this one. I was working in a dance club as a bartender—"

"I was a mobster who left the life to play piano in your bar," he finished.

"Yes," she said, feeling absolutely completed. "You had the same dream."

"More than that," he said.

"Really? You've dreamt about our other lives?" she asked, mystified. "Tell me about them."

"They're only bits and pieces but I've dreamt about us living in times and places all over the world," he said. "We've been painters in fifteenth century Vienna, nobles in ancient Egypt, a politician and a prostitute in ancient Greece—"

"A prostitute?" she blurted.

"Yes, sorry, they weren't all fairytales." He chuckled. "I think prostitutes were celebrities in those times because you were quite famous."

She pictured it. She supposed it wasn't all that different from certain female celebrities today who use sex to acquire fame. With her powers, it kind of made sense that such a profession would have crossed her path in at least one of her many lifetimes. With her ability to compel and affect men the way she does, she probably barely had to do any real work.

"Maybe it's a good thing I don't remember our other lives together." She laughed.

"I'm glad I've had a chance to see parts of them," he said. "I've seen us meet a hundred times, dance a hundred times, get married, have children, fight, get old. I feel...unbelievably blessed to have a glimpse at our connection to one another. The fact that we are these supernatural beings and have lived thousands of lives is incredible. But to know that, in almost every one of our lives, we somehow manage to find each other—"

He didn't finish his thought. He didn't need to. They had a deeper connection than just being Fire and Water. They didn't dream about Lily or Skylar, at least she hadn't. So it didn't seem that all four of them found each other in each life. Just she and Sebastian were bound to one another as much as their elements were bound to them.

The buzzing inside her had been growing all night, and she was quite aware of it now. It felt as if her soul was spreading, growing, and radiating from her. She could almost see a sort of amber glow on her arms. Come to think of it, she could just barely make out a similar teal-tinged glow emanating from Sebastian. Even through the illusion he created, she saw it. She felt more connected than ever to him. She felt this glow from him—a kind of palpable spiritual matter which was cool, refreshing, and placating. She wondered if he felt her aura, and if it felt hot and out of control to him.

"Tell me more about our lives together," she said. "I wanna know everything."

As they swayed back and forth and more music played, he told her stories about what he'd dreamt. She let his words paint pictures inside her head and push out all the worry of what tomorrow would bring.

"Here, the rest is yours," Lily said to Phoenyx, passing her what was left of the apple—a core with the slightest bit of fruit left.

Phoenyx took the apple and nibbled what she could. *Oh, please let this work so I can get some real food!* The desperation alone would be enough to turn her into a vicious ass kicker. She discarded the apple and stood, inviting everyone else to stand up with her.

"Is everyone ready?" she asked. "There's no

turning back once we open that door." The three of them nodded, then all took in a deep breath. "All right, Skylar, open the bars."

Skylar turned to the bars dividing the room. Bending and twisting like they were nothing more than oversized twist ties, the bars in front of both cells spread wide apart with a loud metallic whine. Phoenyx stepped out and over the low horizontal bar, then took Lily's hand to help her out as the boys got out of their cell.

As they approached the door, Phoenyx trembled all over. This was the first time in a week she was able to take more than five steps in any one direction and her legs felt unstable beneath her, loose like overcooked spaghetti. Then there was the fact that they might be walking right into their doom.

"Is there anyone on the other side of the door?" Sebastian whispered to Skylar.

Skylar tilted his head to listen. "There are three people surrounding the door," he whispered. "One on either side of the door against this wall and one standing a few feet in front of it, against the opposite wall. Sebastian, get on my right, Phoenyx on my left, and Lily—you're in the middle behind me. Now, as soon as I open that door, be ready to use whatever means necessary. Ready?"

The group got into formation. Skylar took in one last deep breath, then the door quickly unlocked and swung open. The four of them rushed out.

The two men on either side of the door were thrust far backward down either ends of the hall by an invisible force. The man guarding the front of the door raised a large, long black gun. He aimed it at Skylar's chest and pulled the trigger. What came out was not a bullet but a strange long silver dart with a short, thin tip at one end and a fluffy red feather at the other. The dart slowed and stopped a few inches from Skylar's chest. It then did an about face and zoomed at the trigger man's chest, knocking him out almost instantly.

"Everyone, be careful," Skylar admonished, still and reserved like always, as if he hadn't just been shot at. "That was a tranquilizer. All of their guns have them."

"Tr-tranquilizers are v-very unstable," Lily stuttered, much more shaken but still a river of knowledge. "They affect everyone differently and a-at different rates. Just because they don't knock you out right away d-doesn't mean they won't affect you. We got lucky that it hit him so fast." She looked in Sebastian's direction and gasped. "Huh! Sebastian, look out!"

Sebastian spun around in time to face the guard who was flung from his side of the hall earlier and now came at him in a fury. He swung a fist at Sebastian's head. Sebastian swooped down out of reach, then came back up with his own fist right under the man's jaw, forcing the man to stumble backward in pain. Sebastian bent his leg up and kicked him in the gut, throwing the man to the floor. When the man was on his back, Sebastian stomped over, ripped the gun away from him, and shot him in the chest.

This one wasn't going down as easily as the first. Snarling, he lifted himself up and, out of reflex, Sebastian spun the gun in his hands and smashed the butt against the man's face, knocking him out.

"My element may not be useful in a fight but years of practice on the mean streets of Vegas sure are," Sebastian said.

No sooner had the words come out of his mouth than strong, hard arms bound Phoenyx from behind. Before she knew what was happening, the arms flung her hard against the wall, shooting piercing pain all up and down her right arm where it made contact. She screamed out. She didn't have time to give in to the pain, for the man came at her again, hands open and aiming for her neck.

She reached up her left hand and intercepted him as quickly as she could, gripping his meaty arm firmly and yelling, "Stop!"

The man froze in an attack stance above her. Trembling and panting, she let go of his arm and crept out from under him, staring at him the whole time. Not a single part of him moved—he wouldn't even blink. She had compelled him to stop to the fullest meaning of the word. She didn't even realize she was using her power, it just happened instinctively.

"Are you okay?" Sebastian asked Phoenyx with concern on his face.

The pain shot through her right arm again. She winced and yelped. "No! I think my arm is broken."

Lily rushed to Phoenyx's side and gently moved her fingers up and down Phoenyx's arm. When Lily found the break a few inches above the elbow, Phoenyx cried out again. Lily put her hands lightly around that part of Phoenyx's arm. Phoenyx felt a funny crawly feeling inside her arm. She imagined her bone reattaching itself and sprouting new fibers to mend the break. In seconds, the pain stopped and it felt as though it never was injured.

"Oh, thank you!" Phoenyx exclaimed, throwing her arms around Lily. "I told you we needed you. You don't know how much that hurt! I would have been in serious shit if you couldn't heal me."

"Any time," Lily said in faux nonchalance. "Just, please, no one else get hurt."

Sebastian and Phoenyx laughed nervously.

Skylar bent to pick up the gun from the unconscious man and handed the gun to Lily. "You need one of these more than any of us."

Taken aback, Lily accepted it with quivering hands. She looked awkward holding it.

"What are we going to do with him?" Sebastian asked, gesturing to the still statuesque attacker.

Phoenyx turned to the man and put her hand on him again.

"Relax now," she commanded.

The man lowered his arms and shoulders and stood in a relaxed position. He looked at her as if she were the only person on the planet who mattered.

"Tell me your name," she ordered.

"Bruce Livingston," he answered enthusiastically.

Angry for the fact that he attacked her and broke her arm, she felt some form of penance was necessary. "Bruce, I want you to slap yourself in the face as hard as you possibly can."

Without pause, he lifted his hand and slapped the side of his face with a loud *clap!* His hand left his cheek bright pink, which soon turned to red.

"Good," she said. "Now, you are going to lead us out of here in the safest route possible. If anyone gets in our way, you will defend each and every one of us with your life." She tightened her grip on his arm and let her will flood into him as she spoke. "Got it?"

"Yes, mistress" Bruce said devotedly.

She rolled her eyes. "My name is Phoenyx. Now, come on and get us out of here." She let go of his arm.

Bruce nodded and headed for the hall to the left, gun raised and ready to shoot. As they followed, stepping over the man Sebastian knocked out, Sebastian said to her, "You're so hot when you take control like that." He slipped her a quick peck on the cheek. Funny how such a simple thing as a kiss on the cheek could give her the pip in her step she needed right now.

****

The hallways they walked through were all made out of cobblestone—the floors, the walls, the ceiling. Every threshold was an archway, making Phoenyx certain this was all quite old. Not to mention that what illuminated the hallways were lanterns with actual flames in them rather than light bulbs; it made everything so dim after days with the blinding fluorescents overhead that she could hardly see her nose in front of her face. They passed by more cement doors like the one that kept them prisoner. She wondered who else was kept down here.

"Where are you taking us?" she asked Bruce, keeping pace behind him.

"To the stairs," he replied.

"The stairs?" Lily asked.

"Yes, we are three stories underground," Bruce said. "We will go up three flights of stairs, all of which are not consecutive so we have a lot of walking to do, then we take the service passage to the kitchen where we will go out through the back. The kitchen only operates for dinner so there shouldn't be anyone there for several hours."

"Are there many more guards like you?" Phoenyx asked.

"Yes, there are thirty-seven security guards patrolling the premises. With the ritual tomorrow, members from all over the world have come. As soon as someone realizes you are out, they will all come after us."

"Well, then I guess we'd better be quick," she said. "Just for curiosity's sake, where are we?"

"The Four Corners Lodge," he answered.

"Yeah, we kinda gathered that," Sebastian said. "Where is the lodge located?"

"Salt Lake City, Utah," Bruce said.

"We're in frickin' Utah?" Sebastian exclaimed. "That's like a nine hour drive from Vegas, and even longer from LA and Seattle."

"Salt Lake City?" Phoenyx asked.

"Yes, the Lodge is one of the oldest buildings in town," Bruce said. "Well, the underground tunnels connected to it, anyway. The above ground stories have been an ongoing work in progress."

She was going to ask more questions about the cult or whatever they called it but, at the end of the hall, a man emerged. When he saw them, he turned the other way and ran out of sight.

"Stop him," Skylar shouted. "He's going to alert the others that we've escaped!"

"It's too late for that," Bruce said as Phoenyx and Sebastian braced themselves to run after him. "We all have ear-pieces; he's already reporting your escape. We have to move, quickly!"

Their pace turned into a jog as they zigzagged through the hallways. They made it to a narrow stairway of carved stone. They hurried, pausing at the threshold to make sure the coast was clear. When Bruce decided it was safe, they rushed into the hall with him at the front of the pack. As soon as they turned the corner, they ran into a group of guards heading their way, all of whom raised their guns instantly and shot at them.

"No," Skylar shouted and threw his hand out in front of him. With that, a roar of wind rushed at the attackers, throwing them hard against the wall behind them. The darts they shot at the escapees deflected back their way and hit them not long after.

"Quick, back this way!" Bruce barked, herding them in the direction they had come and through another series of passages. Then he turned into a niche and opened a door. "In here. They won't expect us to go this way."

"Why is that?" Phoenyx asked as they ran in after him. "Oh," she said, faltering as she saw where they were, an answer no long required.

They were in a large square room with a very tall vaulted ceiling. The floor was made of blocks of stones, with a mosaic of different colored marble in the middle to make a huge version of the symbol their captors wore. This room looked as old as the passages they'd been running through, except for a few terrifying modern accessories. Sitting on top of the giant mosaic symbol were four hospital style gurneys, complete with arm, leg, and chest restraint straps. Each was topped with a metal helmet connected to wires dangling down and grouping up next to an altar-looking thing with a giant lever on the top.

All four of the prisoners stopped cold and stared in horror at their surroundings.

"This is where you were going to do it," Sebastian said, aghast.

"These were going to be our death beds," Skylar said.

"Oh, my God!" Lily gasped.

Instinctively, Phoenyx turned to comfort Lily but was stopped by a detail she should have noticed before—a dart was stuck in Lily's shoulder.

"Oh no, Lily," Phoenyx said in a defeated tone as she pulled the dart out.

Lily's eyes widened in fear as she stared at the dart in Phoenyx's hand. They were filled with a look of doom, a realization that death was so very close.

"It must have somehow gotten through when I deflected them just now," Skylar said.

"What do we do?" Lily whimpered. "When this stuff takes effect, I'll be dead weight."

"I can carry you," Bruce said. "Phoenyx, you'll have to take her gun."

"Okay, good plan," Phoenyx said. "It's gonna be okay, Lily. We're gonna get you out of here in no time. Then we'll get you to a hospital. Everything is going to be okay, I promise."

Lily nodded, her face puckering.

"Come on, let's go," Bruce said.

Phoenyx took the gun from Lily. They ran across the torture room and through another door into another hallway. By the time they got into the hall, Lily stumbled and fell to her knees.

"Shit; she won't make it any farther," Phoenyx said, swooping under one of Lily's arms and pulling her up with her shoulders. "Bruce, you have to take her now. Can you still shoot that thing with one hand?"

"Of course," he said. He picked Lily up and threw her limp little body over his right shoulder, holding the gun in his left hand.

"Phoenyx," Lily murmured, her voice soft and sleepy.

"Lily?" Phoenyx asked, lifting up Lily's face. She was already gone. "I'm going to get you out of here," Phoenyx promised, letting Lily's face down slowly. "All right, let's go," she said to the others.

They made it to the second stairway, narrowly dodging a small band of guards who descended just before and went down the opposite hallway. They ran up.

"The last staircase is a straight shot down the hall," Bruce said. "Then the service entrance is the swinging white door to the far left once we are on the ground floor."

They made it up the stairs and onto the last underground floor. Immediately a shot was fired from the left. A guard waited for them against the wall of the staircase entrance. He shot a dart into Bruce's neck. Bruce swiftly turned and shot back at him. Skylar threw an air burst at him but not before the guard fired a final shot back. Skylar wasn't fast enough to stop the dart from zooming into his chest.

"The prisoners are on B1." The guard coughed as he pressed the bud in his ear.

Skylar and Bruce yanked out their darts. Bruce went to the guard and kicked him in the head. The resulting crack insinuated that the guard was now dead.

"They're all headed this way now," Bruce said, covering his own ear-piece to listen. "Most of them are below us. If we move quickly, we might have a chance before the tranks kick in."

"No," Skylar said. "Phoenyx, Sebastian, you two have to go on without us."

"No," Phoenyx rejected the idea.

"No, I'm not leaving without you," Sebastian asserted.

"You have to," Skylar said. "With Bruce, Lily, and me shot, there's no way we're all getting out of here together. They can't perform the ritual without all four of us. As long as at least one of us gets away, they can't kill us yet. You two get out and get help, then come back for us. It's the only way."

"I promised Lily—" Phoenyx began.

"The only way to keep your promise is to go now," Skylar yelled. "We don't have time to argue. Bruce and I will hold them off with the time we have left."

Phoenyx bit her lip, struggling to make a decision.

"You said the service entrance is on the far left after the stairs?" Phoenyx asked Bruce begrudgingly.

"Yes, then the kitchen is the last door on the right," he said.

"Okay. Take good care of my friends," she ordered.

"With my life," he said, putting his free fist over his heart. Then he set Lily down gently and faced the stairway entrance, ready to fight.

"Skylar—" Sebastian said.

"See you when you get back," Skylar cut him off. "Since I won't be there to watch your back, try not to get into any trouble while you're gone. I don't wanna be kept waiting down here because you got yourself arrested." He smiled a good-bye smile, then turned his back on them and faced the stairs.

"Come on," Phoenyx urged Sebastian. She took his hand and squeezed it tight. They ran down the long, straight hallway together.

She felt his reluctance at leaving Skylar, because it was the same as her own. Neither of them could bear the thought of leaving Skylar and Lily behind but they had to. They were going to get out and find help. They would go to the police station and report this deranged fraternity and come back with a handful of cops, guns blazing. All these psychos would be arrested. Then the four of them could go home.

They ran up the final staircase and through a door leading to a wide open reception hall of modern architecture, with white stuccoed walls and red carpeting. The room was empty.

"The white door!" Sebastian said to Phoenyx, frantically pointing and pulling her to the swinging door to their left.

They pushed the door open and peered down the hall. Then they sprinted down the slippery white linoleum, past windows that let in the first real sunlight they'd seen in so long, to the last door on the right.

They charged into the kitchen, sliding on the slippery floor to the right into a rack of pots as they did so. The pots clanged and rattled obnoxiously, alerting a man washing dishes at the sink against the wall in the center of the room to their presence. The man turned to them, as if expecting to see someone else— another guard perhaps—and his eyes and mouth popped open when he saw it was them. He dropped his dishes and put his hands up in surrender.

Sebastian thrust his arm out toward the sink full of steaming water. The water leapt up and splashed the man in the face, turning his skin instantly red. The man screamed in pain from the heat and ran, blind and bumbling, to the exit door at the back of the kitchen, showing them right where to go. They were almost out!

Phoenyx leapt over the first counter top in her way. Before Sebastian could follow, she heard a shot from behind her and turned around. A black clad guard stood in the doorway, anchoring the swinging door with his gun aimed at Sebastian. A dart stuck out of Sebastian's chest. He pulled it out and swung up a fast leg to kick the gun out of the guard's hands. Angered, the guard dove at Sebastian and tackled him to the floor.

"No," Phoenyx yelled, lifting herself back up over the counter to rescue him.

Sebastian groaned between struggles. "Get out!"

She stopped dead. Leaving Sebastian behind was the absolute last thing she wanted to do. Her heart wouldn't let her. She stared at Sebastian and his combatant for a few very slow seconds, caught between wanting to save him and wanting to get help.

"*Go,*" Sebastian yelled at her, gaining an upper hand against his assailant.

His words took control of her body and she ran for the exit, hating herself with every step. She would come back for him—for all of them.

She ran headlong for the door at the back with the red glaring exit sign above it beckoning her. She hurtled over counters, past baking racks, and finally shoved the door open. Fresh air crashed into her face like a wave on the shore. Sunlight flooded the outside world and enveloped her—welcoming her.

Her feet were on paved black tar—a parking lot with nothing but a dumpster in sight before the brick wall that only barely separated this horrible place from the rest of the world. She darted to the dumpster, slammed the lid down closed, and heaved herself on top of it to jump over the wall.

She landed on an alley of dirt. She made it! She was free! She took a moment to let the endorphins flood as she reveled in her liberation. It never felt so good to be outside, to breathe in cool fresh air, to feel dirt on her hands.

She stood and dusted herself off. Now she had to get to the police. She ran out of the alley and onto a sidewalk alongside a main road. She looked up and down the road, trying to decide which direction to go, which direction might lead to the police station.

Then, not too far down, she spotted a police car parked on the side of the street. *What luck!* She thanked her lucky stars as she ran to the cop car.

The front passenger window was down and the officer in the driver's seat was drinking a cup of coffee and reading a newspaper.

"Officer, I need your help!" She panted, placing her hands on the window sill to brace herself as she tried to catch her breath.

The officer put down his newspaper and looked at her with a startled expression.

"Geez, you scared the crap out of me," he said. "What's the problem, miss?"

"That lodge down the street." She panted. "They're all crazy! They had me and my friends locked up for days. I escaped but my friends are still trapped in there. Please, you have to believe me!"

He looked at her for a minute, mulling over what she said. She wasn't sure if he believed her or not.

"All right, I'll take you to the station and we'll sort this out," he said. He leaned over and opened the passenger door. "Get in."

She slid in and closed the door.

"Thank you so much!" she gushed as she pulled her seat belt on. "You don't know how terrified we've been."

Suddenly, all the doors locked.

The sound made her pause and she looked sideways at the cop. Before she could stop him, his left hand pushed a wet rag up to her face, covering her nose and mouth. She instinctively grabbed his hand, ready to will him to stop but her frantic breathing only sucked in the chloroform faster. She passed out.

Phoenyx sleepily opened her eyes. Soft orange-yellow sunlight flooded her vision. She blinked and saw a wonderfully familiar ceiling above her. She sat up, her hands sinking into the cool fluffiness of her old down comforter. She was in her bedroom, her old bedroom, in the house in Phoenix she grew up in. *Is this real?*

Wait. She remembered. This house burned down years ago and she had caused it. Then it all came rushing back to her. Being trapped in a cell for days, the hunger, the discomfort, her friends, their powers...but she couldn't be alarmed. Not right now. The place she was in right now was the epitome of comfort, warmth, and contentedness. All those worries were so far away.

She stood and walked around her old room, touching all of her old treasures that were lost six years ago. Her Nancy Drew books on the bookshelf, her now much too small clothes hanging in the closet, her NSYNC poster—everything was just as she left it.

She ventured down the stairs slowly, running her hand down the smooth wooden banister, savoring every sensory detail. As she descended, she saw her father sitting at the dining room table, reading the newspaper, and bathed in thick golden sunshine raining through the window. Her memories of him all this time hadn't done him justice. He was so handsome, a beacon of all good things, a halcyon.

He looked at her and smiled. "Hey kiddo. Wow, look at you. My little girl turned into such a beautiful young lady."

The resonating sound of her dad's voice brought tears to her eyes.

"Daddy?" she asked. "Is it really you?"

"It sure is, honey," he said.

She ran down the rest of the steps. He stood up to receive her as she dove into his arms, hugging him as tightly as she could. His arms engulfed her; his embrace the safest place in the world.

"I'm so sorry, Daddy." She wept.

"For what, kiddo?" he asked, pulling her away enough to see her face.

"It's my fault that you're dead," she cried. "I started that fire. I'm a freak!"

"You're not a freak, honey," he said soothingly. "You're a wonderful, smart, resourceful person, and you have an amazing gift. What happened here was an accident." He held her face in his hands. "I could never blame you for it. The only thing I regret was not being able to be here for you as you grew up. Although, your mom did a fine job raising you without me."

Phoenyx shook her head. "How could you not hate me for it? I hate myself."

"I *love* you, Phoenyx," he said. "I couldn't be more proud of the person you've become. You can't let your fear hold you back anymore. Right now, your friends need you. You can't be afraid to use the gifts you were born with. It's your destiny. Don't run away from it. You have to go back now."

"Go back?" she asked. "No, I can't go back now. I've missed you so much, I don't want to say good-bye yet."

"You don't have to say good-bye," he said. "I'm always with you. I love you, sweetheart."

"I love you, too, Dad."

"Now, wake up, Phoenyx. Wake up. Phoenyx—"

CHAPTER 20

"Phoenyx! Wake up!" It was Sebastian's voice.

Phoenyx snapped awake. She tried to sit up but there was a firm leather strap secured snugly over her chest. She lifted her arms to loosen it only to find that her wrists were bound, and so were her ankles. *Oh God! Oh no!* She woke in that nightmarish ritual room and was on one of those hospital stretchers. *No, no, no!*

"Sebastian!" she yelled out.

"You're awake!" he yelled.

She lifted her head as much as she could to look for him. She saw that the room was filled with hooded figures in maroon robes. Sebastian was on the gurney to her left, but as they were placed perpendicular to each other, all she could see of him was from his chest down.

"Sebastian, I'm so sorry!" she yelled. "I thought I got away! I was so close! Lily, Skylar!" She looked to the stretcher on her right and saw Skylar's torso and feet sticking out. But she couldn't see Lily. Lily must be on the stretcher right behind her.

"They're both still out from the drugs," Sebastian said.

Just then, one of the hooded figures approached Phoenyx with one of those creepy silver metal helmets with all the wires sticking out.

"No! Get away from me," she shrieked, struggling like hell to get loose, but it was no use.

"Fuck you, you crazy bastard!" Sebastian spat at the person approaching him.

The figure roughly placed the helmet on Phoenyx's head, despite her squirming and buckled the straps under her chin. She threw her head up and bit down on the person's hand as hard as she could. A female voice cried out as the hand jerked away, dripping blood onto Phoenyx's shirt. The coppery, warm taste of blood filled Phoenyx's mouth, so she wadded it up with her tongue and spat it at the woman. The woman didn't react any further than the initial cry. She kept fiddling with the wires on the helmet, then walked away.

Then chanting began. All around them, the figures formed a giant circle and started singing words Phoenyx didn't understand. *Probably some weird Celtic crap.*

This is it. We lost. I'm going to die. Will my soul stay attached to Fire? When they steal Fire from my body and put it inside their lunatic leader, will my soul be trapped inside of him, too? I hope not! If I'm going to die, at least I can look forward to one thing— that I will be with my dad again.

One familiar male voice rang out above the others. She looked in that direction, craning her neck and barely seeing his face beneath the stupid clumsy helmet on her head. Dexter, the man from the bar—the leader of this cult. He wore the same maroon colored robe as the others with his hood back to show his face. He stepped up to the altar to give a speech to his followers.

"My brothers and sisters," he announced. "The time has finally come for us to correct the mistake our forefathers made all those centuries ago. No longer will the elements belong to the Bound Ones. No longer will we have to search for the power that is rightfully ours. Today, we take that power back. From this day forward, the power of the elements will forever be bound to the Four Corners!"

With that, he pulled down the large lever. An agonizing, uncontrollable pain surged through Phoenyx's body. Her muscles twitched, twisted, and contorted painfully. The more she fought it, the more it hurt. It was like having the worst Charlie horse in every single muscle in her entire body at the same time.

She heard Sebastian groaning beside her, muffled by the constant and terrifying buzz of the electricity traveling through the wires and into her head. Then just under that, she barely heard Dexter's voice speaking in that same language. How strange how beautiful it was, even as she was being electrocuted. Something inside her responded to it, lifting up inside her. It was a feeling similar to that feeling in your stomach at the highest peak of a rollercoaster ride when you're thrown upward.

She couldn't be sure at first, but it felt like the ground beneath her was rumbling and quaking. She thought it was just the beginning of her soul being ripped apart, but she opened her eyes enough to see the faces of those in front of her. They were faces filled with trepidation, looking around at the ceiling and at each other in questioning dismay. Dust was shaken free and falling from the ceiling. The people in front of her were losing their balance. The earth really was shaking. *Is this an earthquake?*

"Fear not, my brothers and sisters," Dexter said. "This is only Earth's feeble attempt at rebellion. It will be over soon."

Earth? Lily is doing this?

"Lily!" Phoenyx shouted as loud as she could. If Lily woke and realized what she was doing with this power against them, she could stop all this right now— even if that meant killing the four of them in the process. All this time, Lily had the power of the entire Earth inside her. She just might be the most powerful one of them all.

As the rumbling calmed, a breeze picked up, lifting and brushing the material of the robes all around. Soon the breeze turned into a wind, faster and stronger, whipping all around the room. That had to be Skylar, unconsciously fighting back with his element as well.

Sebastian groaned then and the walls shook once more. Again, frightened gasps escaped the hooded crowd. Inside the walls, cracking and banging sounded, and then water streamed through the cracks in between the bricks. A small part of Phoenyx's mind understood that this was Sebastian. He desperately tried to pull all the water around them to his aide and the sounds and shaking of the walls was the force of the water bursting through the pipes inside the walls. The water trickled and streamed slowly, gathering into puddles in places and lifting into the air as it swirled itself into perfectly round balls. The musical sound of the water moving was peaceful as a forest stream but what followed was far from peace. Once elevated, the balls hurled themselves at the hooded figures, swirling around their heads. They gurgled horribly and struggled to free themselves until they drowned and fell dead to the floor.

As the chanting continued and Sebastian's groaning grew louder and more pain-filled, the balls of water lost their vitality and burst like water balloons in loud, defeated splashes. Puddles bubbled up in feeble arms, convulsing in unrecognizable shapes as they tried to form into something useful but their attempts were fruitless.

"It's no use," Sebastian shouted to Phoenyx through gritted teeth. "I can't do it. It has to be you!"

She couldn't feel the fear resulting from his words, because she was already terrified of dying and of all the pain she felt. It had to be her.

"You can do it," Sebastian wailed. The pain was clear in his voice. Phoenyx couldn't bear the sound, or to know that he suffered too. "Don't be afraid!" Sebastian yelled.

Her father's voice rang in her head. *"You can't be afraid. Your friends need you."*

But she *was* afraid. She couldn't push away the very real fear of dying, and she couldn't think around the petrifying pain seizing every fiber of her being. She felt her soul lifting out of her body, responding to the ancient words beckoning it from Dexter's mouth.

It wasn't just her life, her soul. It was Lily, Skylar, and Sebastian too. They were all about to die. Sweet Lily, witty Skylar, wonderful Sebastian. She loved them all more than she ever loved anyone who wasn't related to her by blood. They were the first real friends she ever had. In this week together she had grown closer to them than she had ever done with anyone.

Her soul cried out. She saw the very real and bright energy of her essence lifting out of her body. This was it. This was the end. She was going to die.

A sound more heartbreaking than any she had ever known cut through the air. She knew what it was without having to look. But look she did, in Sebastian's direction, to see the magnificent and shimmering teal of his soul pulling unwillingly out of his body. A blue tendril lifted from within his bound arm and stretched out in her direction. With her own soul, she reached out to touch him.

"I love you, Phoenyx," she heard without hearing.

A memory, hidden deep within her soul, burst to life, pulling her out of the present and into the far, far past.

Suddenly, she was sitting in a sunflower-filled meadow. The lazy afternoon sun bathed her in light and warmth with birds chirping all around. She was wearing a simple gown of white fox fur which was itchy and uncomfortable. But she couldn't scratch. She was not in control of her actions but merely watching through her eyes.

"Adara," a voice she knew called from across the meadow.

She looked up. Sebastian, handsome as ever and adorned in a very primitive tunic of bear skin that was just long enough to cover the important parts, happily waved and approached her.

"Fin!" she said excitedly, jumping to her feet and running into his arms. He caught her and kissed her.

"The elders have made their decision," Fin said, still holding her. "We've been chosen for the ritual!"

"We have?" she exclaimed. "That's amazing! Oh, this is so wonderful!"

"I know! We will be the most respected people in the entire village, and we can finally get married— despite what your father says!"

"Oh, Fin; I love you!" She threw her arms around his neck and kissed him again.

"The ritual will take place tonight," he said. "We have to get back so we can get ready. First, I have something for us." He held out a golden colored apple.

"A quince?" she asked.

"Do you know what is special about this fruit?" he asked.

She shook her head.

"It is said that, if a couple shares this fruit on their wedding night, their love will be eternal." He took a crude-looking blade from a strap on his tunic and sliced the fruit in half. "I know we are not yet wed but, in case the ritual goes wrong tonight, I want to make sure I will see you in the afterlife."

She smiled and took one half of the quince from him. "As far as I'm concerned, our love is already eternal."

They bit into the fruit and did not get up until they had finished both halves. Then they hurried back to the village.

Everyone was atwitter, bustling about their huts and chatting excitedly about the ritual. When Adara and Fin passed by, all eyes were on them and filled with reverence. What an honor this was! She would be host to one of the great elements.

She did not understand the elders' need to contain the elements, though. The elements, in all their power, made the world they live in—through both destruction and creation, death and life. It was a cycle and she understood that. Perhaps by allowing one of the elements to enter her, she could give it a sort of new life and a balance. She hoped she would be able to do justice to whichever element she was bonded with.

"Adara, come," an aged but still fair woman beckoned. "We must get you ready for the ritual."

"Yes, Mother," she said obediently, leaving Fin and following her mother back to their hut. There, her mother and sister cleaned her thoroughly by scrubbing every inch of her. Then they clothed her in the finest cloth and covered her with sweet smelling flower wreaths. They brushed and braided her hair and stuck flowers all through it. She had never been so pampered in all her life.

"You are ready, my daughter," her mother said, cupping her face.

"You look beautiful," her sister said adoringly.

"I will honor you, Mother—and Father, too," she said.

By the time they left their hut it was night and the bright and full moon was making its way up from the horizon. The moon was so very large tonight which was the only reason the ritual would be allowed to work. They met everyone else at the center of the village, where all were gathered in a circle. The crowd spread to allow her to enter the circle where Fin and the two other chosen candidates were being prepared by elders. Fin knelt next to a giant oblong stone that had been hollowed out and filled with water. Skylar's ancient doppelganger knelt next to a tall structure built out of wood that Phoenyx would now recognize as a gallows, with a noose hanging from it. Lily's ancient counterpart knelt next to a burial pit about her size.

All of these things frightened Adara. She didn't look forward to what awaited her.

"This way, child," one of the lady elders said, taking her arm and guiding her to the fourth corner where a pile of kindling sat, begging to be burned.

Adara understood. Each of the four chosen ones were matched with an element, and it appeared they would have to be harmed by their element in some way during the ritual. The hanging rope made that obvious. The blond boy would be hung and she assumed that he would be bound to Air. When hung, he would be surrounded by only air, and the inability to breath would be air doing harm to him, however inadvertently. The pretty brunette girl would be buried alive, therefore being hurt by Earth. It frightened her terribly that Fin would be held under that water in the hollowed stone and drowned. That left Fire for her.

Will I be burned alive? Adara thought. *How will any of us survive these horrors?*

The lady elder brought by a torch and lit the kindling before Adara.

"On this night," the most powerful of the village sorcerers began, "we will free ourselves from the tyranny of the elements. No longer will earth deny us our crops. No longer will the seas deny us sail. No longer will wind dishevel our homes. No longer will the fire hold sway over our lives." He gave a nod to the elders standing by each of the four volunteers.

At the elders' bequest, Fin climbed into the stone tub, the blond boy fastened the rope around his neck, and the brown haired girl carefully lowered herself into the burial pit with bleeding hands, bringing a cloth with which to cover her pretty face. Then the elder next to Adara handed her a rather blunt blade.

"When the ritual begins and you hear the chanting, cut your hand and drip the blood into the fire," the elder woman said.

Adara took the blade, feeling like she got off easier than everyone else. The other three were actually putting their lives in danger, whereas all she had to do was bleed a little. That was the catch, wasn't it. All three of the other elements could harm a person without causing permanent or lethal damage; but fire doesn't just harm, it destroys completely. This was the only way fire could hurt her without causing her serious damage. She whispered a silent prayer for Fin's safety before the elder leader started the ritual.

Doing as she was told, Adara sliced the dull blade deep into her open palm, biting her lip against the throbbing pain of it, then held it out over the burning fire in front of her. All around them, the village chanted words she had not yet learned, the language of the ancient runes. As she held out her bleeding hand, she watched in anxious fear as the blond boy's face turned red while the rope pulled him upwards off his feet by the neck. The elder to her right piled dirt into the burial pit on top of the brown haired girl. Her beloved Fin struggled against the arms that held him under the water, drowning him.

She made to go to him but the elder woman at her side stopped her. "You mustn't, child. The ritual is not complete. Concentrate on your hand, concentrate on the fire. Let it fill you."

Taking one last stricken and longing look at Fin's flailing hands, she put all her focus on her hand and the fire and prayed that this would end soon.

The chanting around her caused a stir in the air. The earth rumbled. She heard the distant shores clashing with waves. The fire in front of her spun in an unusual fashion. It mesmerized her, drowning out all other sounds and sights, and she watched the flames dance and flicker and reach up to lick at her dripping blood. The chanting grew louder and faster, and the fire grew taller and brighter. She quivered and felt as though the fire tugged at her soul.

Then suddenly, in the loudest silence, the chanting came to a rude halt. The air went still, the water hushed, the earth calmed, and the fire drew itself up into her hand before snuffing itself out and stealing all the light with it.

Drawing in a deep breath as if fighting suffocation, she felt the heat of the fire enter the cut in her hand and burn up her arm and into her chest and all through her body. However, it wasn't a sweltering, blistering, or even uncomfortable heat—just merely warm and relaxing, the way the heat of the sun soaks into your muscles on a hot summer day. She felt triumphant but also deeply sad. She felt reborn.

Something sparked inside of Phoenyx suddenly as the memory faded and she snapped back to the present—something that stabbed through the pain and the fear. It started as an ember in her stomach and grew and grew. Anger. Rage. Hatred. These people think they can do whatever they want because of their heritage. They had the arrogance, the hubris centuries ago to trap the elements so that they could control them and become masters of the world they lived in and depended on. Because of them, Phoenyx's element, Fire, had to live time and time again, never allowed to rest, never allowed to be free. Life after life, death after death, forced to repeat over and over again. It wasn't just her anger and hatred for what these people had done to her and her friends that she was feeling, it was Fire's anger and hatred for what these people had done to it and the other elements long ago and what they were trying to do yet again.

In that moment, she and Fire were of one mind. Fire refused to be ripped from the body it made its home. It refused to belong to its enslavers. It would not stand for this any longer. After all this time, Fire was going to have its revenge.

In an eruption of hatred and retaliation, Phoenyx screamed at the top of her lungs, letting Fire take over. She felt the heat inside her body reach out like magma spewing from the mouth of a volcano and scorching all her enemies. Even with her eyes squeezed tightly shut, she saw all the hooded figures being lit aflame from within, burning rapidly as they screamed short-lived screams, blackening and charring, and then falling to the floor in ashes.

She opened her eyes and looked at the straps that bound her. Without even having to voice the thought in her head, flames sparked and ate away at them, freeing her arms to remove the wretched electrifying helmet.

Dexter was the only figure left still standing and he was gawking at Phoenyx in horror like a deer in the headlights. She stepped over to the altar and pulled the lever back up, cutting off the electricity, and Dexter ran for the nearest door. Phoenyx brought up tall flames to block the door, then the others that Dexter ran for, and so on until the entire room was encircled by a wall of fire. Dexter had nowhere to go.

She waved her hand at the stretchers in an order for the others' straps to singe away. As soon as Sebastian was free, Phoenyx heard him kick his stretcher angrily and go to the aide of Skylar and Lily.

Phoenyx approached Dexter and grabbed his arm, digging in her nails into his flesh.

"Please, Fire, kill me quickly," he begged, closing his eyes in preparation of death.

"No," she said. "You don't get off that easy. You don't deserve a quick death. You deserve to suffer." She let her will flow through her hand and into him, and said, "You will never speak again. You will never move again. You will see nothing and you will hear nothing for the rest of your life. You will be a shell of your despicable self and you will have to suffer for the rest of your days with the shame and guilt of what a terrible person you are until it eats you alive."

She let go and his eyes did not follow her. He was a statue, just as the guard had been when she'd frozen him by accident, only Dexter was going to stay this way forever. With a flick of her wrist, she pushed her index and middle fingers against his chest, and he fell straight backward till he slammed harshly to the floor, stiff as a board.

"Come on buddy, wake up," she heard Sebastian urging Skylar, followed by the sound of slaps on cheeks.

Phoenyx took a moment to let her anger fade and to remember herself, letting Fire return to its den deep within her soul to savor its vengeance. Then she turned and joined Sebastian in recuperating their friends.

"Honey, wake up," she said, shaking Lily's shoulders lightly. "Oh, duh," she said to herself, remembering that she could *make* Lily wake up. "Wake up," Phoenyx said, compelling Lily.

Lily's pretty green eyes opened. Her face brightened when she saw Phoenyx's face hanging over hers.

"You came back," she said to Phoenyx.

"Of course, I did," Phoenyx said.

"Hey, Phoenyx, could you work your magic on Skylar, too?" Sebastian asked.

"Yeah, sure," she said, going to awaken Skylar.

"Oh, my God, what happened?" Lily gasped as she looked around at all the ash covered robes and the wall of flames around them.

"You don't remember anything?" Phoenyx asked as Skylar stirred.

"I don't either," Skylar grumbled. "All I know is I have the biggest headache of my—holy hell!" He cut himself off when he opened his eyes.

"Long story short, they caught us all, nearly electrocuted us to death. Phoenyx scorched all their asses," Sebastian said. "If I hadn't been seizuring at the time and my spirit wasn't being torn from my body, it would have been the coolest thing I've ever seen. See, Phoenyx, I knew you could do it. You saved us."

Phoenyx felt Skylar reading her mind. Odd, she was never aware of it before. He was looking for scenes of what happened.

"Whoa, you're one scary bitch, you know that," he said to Phoenyx. "Don't ever change."

She smiled, then took note of how weak her body was despite how strong she felt. Her knees were weak, her legs were shaky, and her stomach felt like she'd be throwing up right now if she had anything to throw up.

"So…it's over?" Lily asked. "We're free?"

"Yes, we're free," Sebastian said, helping Lily to her feet.

"Let's get the hell out of here," Phoenyx said.

"First things first, we all need a shower," Sebastian said. "Some of us more than others." He pointed at Skylar. It was amazing that he could resort right back to humor after being almost killed.

As the boys argued, Phoenyx let the flame wall die down. They all headed slowly out of the room and to the stairs. Her first thought was that they needed to go to the hospital but her stomach demanded priority, and a giant meal sounded way too good right now.

They walked out of the empty lodge, hand in hand, and into a fresh and beautiful late morning. This felt like the first day of a new life, and the possibilities were endless.

CHAPTER
21

"Do I really have to get in there?" Phoenyx complained.

"Yes, you do," Sebastian said. "You promised. Although, I have to admit, I'm loving just looking at you in that bikini."

She stuck her tongue out at him. Then she sucked in a breath and held it as she dipped her toe into the bubbling hot water. It actually felt not totally horrible, so she let her foot fall farther and farther until it was flat against the first step of the hot tub.

"Come on, Phoenyx, just take the leap and get all the way in," Skylar encouraged, sitting across from Sebastian with his arms resting back on either side of the top of the tub.

Sebastian grabbed her hand and pulled her in, gracefully and easily spinning her to catch her on his lap. The splash of the warm water on her legs and stomach sent goose bumps all over but the fact that she was on Sebastian's lap made up for the felinic discomfort of being partially submerged.

"You are such a brat!" she whined.

"Aha, but admit it, this isn't as bad as you thought it would be," he said.

She shrugged.

"Well then, let me make you more comfortable," he said. He held one side of her face and kissed her.

Oh, those lips could dissolve all the tension in the world. She gave in eagerly, instantly wanting more. They had not had any alone time together since escaping yesterday morning, and the one thing she still wanted more than anything had yet to be attained.

After they left the lodge, they first went to a diner and ate until they were all sick. Then they decided it would be best to go to the hospital and get themselves checked out. There was no way they could tell anyone what actually happened to them—"we were kidnapped and tortured by a secret society that tried to steal our powers from us because we are the four elements in living form." No, they'd all get thrown in a loony bin, and it would just call a bunch of unnecessary attention. No reason to get the cops involved in a threat that was already eradicated. So they came up with a story encompassing all the bad things they'd gone through so the doctors would know what to look for, but that wouldn't cause any trouble: they all went to some party, got drunk, had something slipped into their drinks—to give an explanation for the tranquilizers and chloroform they'd all been given. Then, while they were in a pool, someone accidentally kicked a radio in and they got shocked—to give an explanation for them all having been partially electrocuted. The effort of making up the lie and going to the hospital had been wasted because they all turned out to be fine, save for being abnormally malnourished, and the doctors lectured them about drinking less and eating more.

After a few hours at the hospital and a while preparing what they were going to say, Phoenyx and Lily both called their parents. As she suspected, Phoenyx's mom had no idea there was anything wrong. She had been slightly concerned that Phoenyx hadn't returned her three phone calls but assumed Phoenyx was just having a lot of fun meeting new people and getting settled in.

Lily's parents were a completely different story; they had totally freaked out. Lily had never been away from home for more than a day before and, in those cases, her parents knew where she was and when she'd be home. Lily had been gone for over a week and they had no idea where she was or what could have happened to her. Naturally her parents had the cops going crazy looking for her.

So Lily made up a quite ingenious excuse. Apparently, she had pledged a fancy sorority on campus and, as initiation, the sorority kidnapped all the pledges and took them to a camp where they were put through a week of challenges in which they were not allowed to contact anyone. Lily went along with it because this sorority would look good on her resume. Her parents would be pleased to know that the week away from home made her reconsider the sorority and she wouldn't join. Lily was an exceptional liar considering that chances were she never lied to her parents before in her life. She told them she would be home in two days.

After all they went through, Skylar and Sebastian thought they all needed a day of fun together to celebrate their freedom, so last night they flew them all first class to Las Vegas to stay in one of their favorite hotels, Caesar's Palace. They promised they would buy the girls a flight home tomorrow, and they spent the day living it up and relaxing. Since this was their last night all together, Phoenyx figured she'd live up to the promise she made to Sebastian the night they met. Tonight she would make sure they had some time alone, in his room.

"All right, I got the champagne," Lily said, coming over to the hot tub in her adorable little purple bikini with a skirt bottom, carrying a bottle of champagne in one hand and four tiny glasses in the other. She slipped into the tub and sat next to Skylar, and he did the honors of popping it open and pouring a glass for everyone.

"To freedom," Skylar said, raising his glass.

"To being a bunch of extremely good looking, super powerful bad-asses," Sebastian said as he raised his glass, making them all laugh.

"So, wait, you're telling me I actually made the ground shake?" Lily asked after taking a sip.

"Yeah, you did," Phoenyx said. "You scared the hell out of everyone. Who knew you had it in you."

Lily blushed, still unable to get her mind around it. "I just can't believe it."

"I still can't believe I missed it all," Skylar said. "Seeing it through the two of your minds is okay but I would have loved to see them all get what they deserved with my own eyes."

"It doesn't matter now," Sebastian said. "All that matters is we're free and life is beautiful."

"So, what's next for all of us?" Phoenyx asked. "Lily, I know you're going back to college in Seattle."

"Yes but I definitely want to visit you guys on winter break," Lily said. "I'm actually really going to miss you all. Now that we all have working cell phones again, you'd better all text me every day."

They laughed and all assured they would keep in contact.

"My classes start in five days. What about you two, what are your plans?" Phoenyx asked, fishing for an answer about where she stood with Sebastian.

"Well, funny you should mention that," Sebastian said. "Skylar and I were talking last night and we decided...maybe we could both use a bit of an education."

"An education? You mean college?" she asked.

"Yeah, as a matter of fact, UCLA doesn't look too bad," Sebastian said.

"Really? You're going to leave behind a world of riches and luxury in Las Vegas to go to school in LA?" she pressed, trying to hide her hopefulness.

"Yep," Sebastian said with a big smile. "We both have a ton of money saved up and, whenever we need more, it's a short flight from LA to Vegas. I figure I'll study business, or marine biology, or maybe law with how much I get in trouble."

She laughed giddily.

"What are you going to study, Skylar?" she asked.

"I've always had an interest in Physics," he said. "Seeing as we're all a bit of a scientific phenomenon, it might be worthwhile to study."

"Okay, just as long as we don't end up as your test subjects," Lily said.

"I make no promises," Skylar joked.

Phoenyx turned back to Sebastian. "So, you're really doing this? You're going to move to LA and go to school with me?"

"Well, I still owe you that date," he said jokingly, then his face became sincere and his voice hushed so that only she heard. "I only just found you and I'm not ready to let go." He took her hand in his and braided his fingers through hers.

She smiled. "Not that I don't love being in this delightful hot tub, but why don't you and I take this party to your room? We have unfinished business to attend to." She winked at him.

"Well, we have to go now. See you guys in the morning," Sebastian said to Lily and Skylar quite eagerly. He then pulled Phoenyx out of the tub, threw her over his shoulder, and headed to his room.

Laughing exuberantly, Phoenyx waved at Lily and Skylar until they were out of sight. She was ecstatic to finally have Sebastian all to herself.

Visit www.tricia-barr.com for information about Book 2, *Tantric*.

About the Author:

Tricia Barr always loved the written word, however, loving history and the idea of travel more, she pursued a degree in Anthropology. She graduated from the University of Arizona in 2011 and looked hard for a job in her field for two years before she realized that her degree would not allow her the travel opportunities she truly wanted.

Now she works as a writer and a jack-of-all-trades with her husband, Eric Bar, leaving them both plenty of time and freedom to travel on their own terms as they try to start a family.

Visit Tricia Barr online at:

http://www.tricia-barr.com

CPSIA information can be obtained
at www.ICGtesting.com
Printed in the USA
FFOW04n1719010717
37295FF

9 780998 977713